DIETRICH
KALTEIS
TRIGGER
FISH

DIETRICH KALTEIS

TRIGGER FISH

A CRIME NOVEL

ECW PRESS

TORONTO

Published by ECW Press
665 Gerrard Street East
Toronto, Ontario, Canada M4M 1Y2
416-694-3348 / info@ecwpress.com

Cover design: David Gee
Cover photo: © hidesy/iStock
Author photo: Andrea Kalteis

This is a work of fiction. Names, characters,
places, and incidents either are the product of
the author's imagination or are used fictitiously,
and any resemblance to actual persons, living or
dead, business establishments, events, or locales is
entirely coincidental.

LIBRARY AND ARCHIVES CANADA CATALOGUING
IN PUBLICATION

Kalteis, Dietrich, author
Triggerfish / Dietrich Kalteis.

Issued in print and electronic formats.
ISBN 978-1-77041-153-1 (paperback)
ALSO ISSUED AS: 978-1-77090-830-7 (PDF)
978-1-77090-831-4 (EPUB)

I. TITLE.

PS8621.A474T75 2016   C813'.6   C2015-907268-9
C2015-907269-7

The publication of *Triggerfish* has been generously supported by the Canada Council for the Arts
which last year invested $153 million to bring the arts to Canadians throughout the country, and by the
Government of Canada through the Canada Book Fund. *Nous remercions le Conseil des arts du Canada
de son soutien. L'an dernier, le Conseil a investi 153 millions de dollars pour mettre de l'art dans la vie des
Canadiennes et des Canadiens de tout le pays. Ce livre est financé en partie par le gouvernement du Canada.*
We also acknowledge the Ontario Arts Council (OAC), an agency of the Government of Ontario,
which last year funded 1,709 individual artists and 1,078 organizations in 204 communities across
Ontario, for a total of $52.1 million, and the contribution of the Government of Ontario through the
Ontario Book Publishing Tax Credit and the Ontario Media Development Corporation.

Ontario
Ontario Media Development
Corporation

ONTARIO ARTS COUNCIL
CONSEIL DES ARTS DE L'ONTARIO
an Ontario government agency
un organisme du gouvernement de l'Ontario

MIX
Paper from
responsible sources
FSC
www.fsc.org   FSC® C016245

Canada Council
for the Arts

Conseil des Arts
du Canada

Canadä

PRINTED AND BOUND IN CANADA   PRINTING: FRIESENS   1   2   3   4   5

TO ANDIE

. . . HOT LUNCH

"Whoa, you see that?"

Rene Beckman told Danny Green to ease the cruiser around the corner, experienced cop eyes catching a glimpse down the alley. Two guys at the back of the Christian book-store, a van backed to the loading dock, exhaust puffing from its pipe, middle of the night. Seven years on the force, Beck had it down in seconds.

"What's up?"

"Bet you a Starbucks there's no King James in those boxes," Beck said.

Killing the lights, Danny pulled to a stop, Beck getting out.

"Want me to call it in?" Danny said, feeling on eggshells since Beck nailed two seventeen-year-olds playing Knockout last week: rich white kids preying on inner-city down-and-outs, getting kicks and manhood points by throwing fists at some homeless zombies. The game: drop one with a single punch. Leave them face down and walk away laughing.

Cornered the pair in an alley off Abbott, Beck putting his service Glock to the taller kid's temple, letting him hear it click, asking which one's Ali, which one's Frazier. The kid up on his tiptoes, stain spreading across his chinos. Beck telling him about a new game, calling it Shootout, telling the kid it would start next time he laid eyes on him down in this part of town, letting the pair run off.

Turned out the one he dubbed Frazier — one Warwick Preston — snapped a telling shot with his cell phone. The kid's doting parents suing the department for brutality, the papers making a media meal of it, the shot of Beck pressing his service piece to Kenny "Ali" Lange's temple making the front page. The homeless vic faded into the shadows, and Beck was left with only Danny's word, his duty status under review.

Six months out of training, valedictorian of his graduating class at Depot, Danny Green's luck had gone straight into the shitter the day he was assigned as Beck's partner. Backing up every play, he'd been reschooled in looking the other way and keeping his mouth shut, telling the review board no excessive force was used on the two teens playing Knockout, Beck being one righteous cop. Danny knew the kind of career move it would be to say anything different. Six months in, and yeah, Danny was learning the ropes.

That was the second time Beck had been up for review. The first time was on account of the beating he put on a guy a year back for shooting a cat off a tenth-story ledge with a BB gun, greasy fuck sitting in his lawn chair, shooting from the next building over, getting his kicks. With no witnesses, Beck got off clean, but it was different the second time around.

Used to be Beck thought he was taking down crime one asshole at a time, getting it done. But the assholes were springing up faster than the department could put them down, miles of paperwork, review boards and lawyers in pinstripes waiting by their phones.

The worst shit-hole in the country. Seven years working Beat Enforcement, Beck figured they ought to throw yellow tape all around the Downtown Eastside, pull the Listerine drunks from the gutters and find them some housing, stick extra beds in St. Paul's and detox the junkies. Put up shelters for the battered hookers and pass out meds to the crazies. That or watch it all go to hell.

Now, hand on the mike, Danny caught Beck's shadow along the top of the alley. Giving up on calling for backup, he flipped on his cap. He got out and went to the mouth of the alley, asking Beck how he wanted to play it.

"Go that way," was all Beck said, and he took off down the alley. Danny moved along the street — first time he might have to draw his piece, depending what was really happening — felt the sweat under his arms.

Around the east corner of the four-story, Beck unsnapped the holster, his Glock already drawn, safety off. Allowing his eyes to adjust to the dark, he stepped past the garbage, feeling his way along the bricks. At the back corner, he stuck his head out. Light from a streetlamp gave him a bead on the two guys out back of the Jesus Factory, a dark-colored Chevy van backed to the dock, its engine running. The two guys busy loading boxes. A security bulb over the open door, a crowbar against the wall, splintered wood sticking from the jamb, both guys wearing hoodies.

Coming up along the side of the dock with the Glock up, Beck kicked a can with his shoe. Both men turned, one guy dropping his box, hand going under his jacket.

"Wouldn't do that," Beck said, had the guy point blank.

Danny Green came around the other side of the dock, barking, "Police. Freeze." Jumping up the steps, hand on his nightstick, Danny was going by the book, the force-with-force rule about to be his undoing.

The guy still holding the box was shorter, turned to Danny, Danny telling him to set it down. Grabbing the other guy, Beck face-planted him against the bricks, taking his piece, dropping it in his own pocket, saying he wanted to see his hands, yanking his hood off.

The one with the box hesitated as Danny stepped up, hand on the nightstick. Tossing his box at Danny, he let the Converse fly, jumping off the dock and running full out. Danny stumbled over the guns tumbling from the box and went after him.

Snapping on the cuffs, Beck spun his man around, holstering his piece, asking for a name.

"Got them kind of tight," the guy said, meaning the cuffs, smacking gum behind the stupid grin.

Palming the guy's forehead, Beck bounced his skull off the bricks, the gum falling out, Beck asked, "That better?"

The guy lost the cute, saying his name was Baldie Jones, throwing in, "You got no cause . . ."

Bouncing his head again, Beck skipped the Miranda speech, saying he was arresting him for being a thieving dickhead — judging by the spilled guns and crowbar by the door, these two were robbing the real gun runners. Beck heard Danny yelling freeze somewhere down the alley.

In pursuit, Danny sprinted, held the nightstick like he was in a relay race, the suspect refusing the baton. The guy jumped up the chain-link at the end, scrambling over the razor wire, getting ripped up and dropping down the far side.

"I'll shoot," Danny yelled.

"Right here, bee-ach," the guy said with some kind of accent, back-pedalling, grabbing his crotch, laughing and running off.

Staring at the razor wire, Danny heard the guy's feet on the pavement, fucker still laughing. Slipping the stick into his duty belt, Danny walked back, thinking he should have pulled his piece, knowing the shit he'd catch from Beck.

Coming around the corner, the loading dock lit by the single bulb, Danny caught Beck driving a fist into Baldie's middle and folding him up, the guy going to his knees, hands cuffed behind him. Baldie Jones was puking when the figure sprang from the back of the van, Danny yelling, too late.

Beck had his hand on the Glock, turning.

The bulb over the door lit the face — a woman's, dark-skinned, her body pressing into him. He felt the blade go through the Kevlar. Beck grabbed at her, going limp, the breath leaving him, looking into her eyes.

Screaming his name, Danny pulled his piece, the figure turning to him, her hood falling off. Danny fired a wild round, killing the single bulb, the night swallowing the scene. No chance for a second shot. And the woman was gone.

Then Danny was cradling Beck's head, his own Glock down on the dock. "Oh, Christ." Not sure what to do. Fumbling his handset, Danny told Beck to hang on, calling it in.

The guy Beck cuffed wasn't waiting around. Baldie got up and started to run, Danny yelling and grabbing his gun,

5

the Hogue grip kicking in his hand. Put one dead center, dropping Baldie Jones.

Danny barked the 10-33 into the mike. "Officer down." Repeating it.

Spinning down the black hole, Beck caught hold of Danny's arm, forcing the words through the pain, "Uncuff him."

It took a moment, Danny putting it together, nodding, taking off the cuffs and grabbing an AK from a crate, putting it next to the guy, sirens coming past the Woodward's building.

Paramedics rushed Beck off in the ambulance, Danny replaying it for the sergeant on the scene, saying how it went down, FIU snapping photos, a couple more uniforms holding back the late-night looky-loos and news crews.

He told it again downtown. A guy in a suit from the Independent Investigations Office took notes. Looking at his shaking hands, Danny told him it was a woman that stabbed his partner, did his best to describe her. Told how he shot the guy making a play, grabbing for an AK from the spilled crate marked *Lord, Teach Me How.*

Clicking his pen, the investigator closed his notebook, telling Danny it looked textbook, a righteous shoot, clapping Danny's shoulder, telling him to try and get some sleep, hoping his partner pulled through. Going out the door, he said there ought to be a citation in it. Danny feeling like he might puke, looking down between his shoes.

. . . BUST IT, BABY

NOT ANOTHER boat, not a sail, not a kayak in sight, quiet for an early Friday evening. Gulls lined the rock outcrop, squawking like it was a social, a seal poking its shiny head up, porpoising, and was gone.

Waves lapped the hull, clouds milled to the north; light westerlies promised to shower the Georgia Strait.

Checking his course along the west side of Pasley Island, Beck kept her about a hundred feet offshore, Popham just due west, Little Popham to the north. Looked like rain up at Hermit. He tapped his hand on the wheel of his Grady-White, a thirty-two-footer he dubbed *Triggerfish*. His heart was pumping, this girl looking fine, like the Spice Girl that married the soccer star, back in her blonde days. Turned-up nose, bleached hair long in front, cropped in back. The tube top under the designer denim did her justice, shorty shorts, long legs looking oiled. Painted toes in open-toed pumps.

Pumps on a boat.

"Can't say it was any one thing," Vicki Moon was saying, crossing her legs on the aft seat, flipping bangs from her eyes for about the hundredth time, the breeze messing with her do, giving her an untamed look. The girl saying, "Things built up, you know how it goes?"

He said he did, turning to look at her, Vicki sipping her lime girly drink, big rock on her finger, telling him how it ended with her ex. She was checking him out: Beck at the wheel with the ball cap, snug roll-up pants, the linen shirt unbuttoned down to the scar, healed after eight months, an angry jagged line.

"Anyway, if I had to put my finger on it . . ." she said, "it started with Dimples."

"Dimples?"

"Our wiener dog." Her mouth turned into a smile, found her straw and sipped more drink. "Well, his really, his mother's until she passed. Was okay at first, then Dean starts holding her up like she's talking, you know, the way people do with their pets . . ."

"He change his voice, making it cute?" Beck knowing people like that.

"All the time. But nothing cute about it, doing it like that blues guy, John Lee Whoever, making like Dimples was singing."

"Doing how how how and boom boom boom?"

"Yeah." She laughed. "Wiener dog doing the blues." She rubbed her thighs, feeling the chill.

"He do this in front of people?"

"Almost say he lived for it. Family, friends, even took the dog to work. Front of clients, front of everybody."

Beck tried picturing it. White guy doing John Lee Hooker. "Boogie Chillen" coming out of a wiener dog. She recrossed her legs, Beck not wanting her cold.

Vicki saying, "Heard my share of how how hows, let me tell you."

Beck aimed the bow at the cove, the Grady-White bobbing through the light chop, wind picking up a little, pushing the rain over Hermit their way. Barbecuing on the boat was out — nice fillet of spring salmon on ice. Would have been, anyway — she told him she was vegan, said she didn't eat anything that had a pulse.

Told him she knew a vegan place they could get a bite, could go there after.

After.

Pointing out a pod of dolphins feeding on herring, Beck told her the sound was them chuffing through their blowholes. Vicki snapped pics with her cell phone, saying this was going right up on her wall.

Checking her out as she took a shot, Beck was saying, "So Dean doing his John Lee wiener-dog thing, a real mood breaker, huh?"

"You know the final straw?"

"What's that?"

"Dimples liked to watch."

"Watch? As in . . ."

"Uh huh. Real little perv." She looked at him, smiled, then turned and aimed her cell at the dolphins again.

"While you two . . ." He wiggled his fingers, eased up on the throttle.

"Laid right up on the bed, staring the whole way through," she said, tucking the phone in her bag. "Didn't even blink."

"That what they call doggy style?"

"Oh now you're being bad."

He swung the bow into the cove, narrow and curved; pines and cedars lined the rock bank, Beck thinking he'd drop anchor around the bend, take her below. Turn on the heater. Man, this could be epic.

"Anyway, I finally put my foot down, had him put Dimples out."

"Out, as in . . ."

"Not that. Out the French doors, the damn thing yapping and scratching on the other side, clawing at the wood, Dean saying it was messing up his focus . . ." She crooked her finger.

Beck shook his head, steering for the bend.

"Told Dean he was sleeping on the couch, take his wiener with him."

"Teach him a lesson, huh?" Beck said.

"It just got worse. A month of looking at the back of his newspaper over breakfast, Dean got himself a bachelor close to work, place allowing pets. Couple months in he stopped calling, asking if I locked the door, how I was doing; got himself a new girl, met her at Price Chopper. Think he liked the way she didn't speak English."

"But you got over it?"

"What I got was a lawyer, one with razor teeth. Yeah, then I got over it."

Beck nodded, knew how those teeth felt, having been bitten a time or two.

Her mouth found her straw. Finishing the drink, she looked at him, saying, "Getting even's the best part, like therapy. Never having to worry."

Yeah, this would be epic. Spoiled rich girl with the big

rock on her finger. He reached for the Johnnie Walker bottle. Red Label. Unscrewed the cap and took a pull, feeling it burn.

Telling him she did a little acting, nothing big, just enough to kill the boredom, she got up, bopping like there was music. She shrugged out of her denim jacket, letting it drop, eyes closed, hands waving in the air, hips swaying. Putting on a show, dancing to him, she reached around his waist, grinding him into the wheel. "We done talking?"

"Just taking it slow, getting to know each other."

"Slow's okay, long as I don't need to draw you a map."

"Out here we call them charts." Beck slipped his hands to her waist, lips on hers, tasting the lime drink.

Vicki letting it happen, ignoring the Old Spice, plenty of time later, teach him to spritz on some Donna Karan.

When they came up for air she forgot about the cold, Beck taking a last chug from the Johnnie, setting the bottle down. Checking the Lowrance — he had fifty feet under the hull. The carcass of a rowboat against the shore, cedar, pine and rock rimming the cove, no cottages out here. Whitecaps out in the channel, light rain tapping on the canvas top, screeching herring gulls circling.

"Little girl's room?" She pointed below.

"Yeah." Beck nodded, saying, "Duck going down."

"Not fair you boys get to do it standing," she said. Ducking, she went through the twin doors.

Switching to the trolling motor, Beck eased around the bend in the cove, closing the lid on the Weber, one rod still on a rigger. Snapping the line free, he reeled it up, pressed a button and raised the cannonball by the time Vicki was coming back.

Slipping the Hoochie's treble on a guide, he set the rod back in the holder, the dodger fluttering in the breeze. Turning to her, he slid his hands to her hips.

Epic.

"This what you do?" she said. "Get a girl on your boat, take her to a quiet bay?"

"Could tell you you're special."

"Don't need to." Hooking her thumbs on her jean shorts, she considered him, then she undid the snap and pushed them down, could tell the thong was working its magic.

"You like?"

"Red's my favorite color."

"It's raspberry."

Fingers going inside the strap, he walked her to the transom, bumping the fishbox, Beck thinking the last time he was this close to a woman, she stuck a knife in him.

Unlashing his canvas belt, Vicki breathed words in his ear, "Sorry about the vegan thing. Should've warned you."

"No sweat. Got Stouffer's in the box. Mac and cheese, Fiesta Bake, couple more." Beck hurried, fingers feeling clumsy.

Lifting his T-shirt over his head, she let it fall and ran her fingers across his chest, touching the long scar, saving the questions for later, guessing he'd hand her some macho line about nicking himself shaving.

Kicking off his deck shoes, Beck peeled down his roll-ups, didn't mind her looking.

"Commando, nice." Liking that he wasn't shy about it, but thinking a little manscaping wouldn't hurt. Drawing into him, she fished for her handbag, slid her leg up his, whispering, "All hands on Beck."

Snap.

He opened his eyes, her arm outstretched, the cell phone in her hand, pointing at them, snapping a selfie.

"Come on . . ."

Snap.

His hand moved for the cell, Vicki playing keep-away, teasing. "Didn't say cheese."

Snap.

Wrong time for a Kodak moment. He took the cell and tossed it on the aft seat, remembering he hadn't dropped the anchor.

"Just a social media thing we do," she said.

"We?"

"Couple of friends I don't see much."

Fingers at her tube top, he eased her against the helm chair.

Lifting the top over her head, she tossed it on the phone, pulling her shoulders back, letting him look, leaving no doubt she was cold. Kicking off her pumps.

Beck smiled, this girl wearing heels on a boat.

"What's funny?"

He kissed her, forgetting the anchor, forgetting to ask if she wanted to go below, drop the table, pop in the cushions, and . . .

Something caught his eye past the bow and he stopped, looking at a tugboat and some kind of a sub, men with guns, all staring.

. . . SCRATCHING THE SURFACE

RAMON SANCHEZ eased the throttle, the *Mañana* plowing low, the harbor tug leaving its fat wake, entering the cove. Remnants of a wooden hull showed like ribs among a tangle of bramble along the shore, old paint flaking above its water-line. A rock outcrop boxed the cove, plenty deep and hidden from Howe Sound, Ramon motoring up around the bend. Rain to the north.

Eduardo Oliveira Soto went by Eddie. Served as mate on the *Mañana* nearly a year now, pretty much the same time his uncle started moving from the legit work. At the bow rail, he scanned the tea-water ahead of the rubber fenders, watching for deadheads. Anybody cruising on the far side of the rocks would see a tug searching for stray logs to tow. Nothing out of the ordinary.

Cutting his engines, Ramon stuck his head from the cabin, calling, "Okay, ready the anchor."

"You see her?" Eddie looked around.

"Just do it."

Stepping to the windlass, Eddie hit the switch, the chain grinding through the hawsepipe. Glad to be up at the bow.

Didn't need Ramon telling him he looked like shit, hearing how his uncle had paid his dues towing barges, pushing log rafts for better than thirty years, hungover or not. Ramon sounding pissy when he talked like that. Eddie wanting to duck into the head, do a line fat enough to mellow him out.

Scoring an eight-ball off Regular Joe last night at Rudi Busch's lodge out past Hope, Eddie overheard the two Rockers talking, throwing numbers around the pool table, Billy Wall bragging how the Baja Maritano cartel signed up the club, the bikers with visions of West Coast distribution. Regular Joe grinned at that, Joe with the gaunt cheeks and hollow eyes. Eddie watched the guy rail a g in one fat line off the sink in Rudi Busch's can, Eddie thinking it should have knocked the guy over. Nobody did that much in one line. Eddie cutting eight lines from a gram when he started out. Now he cut four, doing more all the time.

This new gig for the Rockers MC was different, running up here instead of taking the tug out to tall water as usual and picking up the dope the crew on the *Sun Sea* pitched off its stern. Ramon and Eddie fishing it out with boat hooks and stashing the loads under the false floor and up in the hidden compartments, bringing it back to the shipyards. Trucking it out to Rudi's lodge. A good payday, Eddie feeding the cravings. Sucking up eight-balls till his nose bled, Eddie trying to deal with the paranoia, thinking cops were around every corner.

Ramon told him to keep watch for the narco sub, the thing built in some Amazon jungle, the bikers starting this new deal with the cartel, the crew subbing it all the way from Mexico, non-stop.

After Uncle DeJesus got nailed in a sweep at the North Shore shipyards nearly a year back, Eddie's habit had doubled, the paranoia growing along with it. His uncle was serving his stretch in Kent for the case of auto weapons and twenty keys of blow the combined forces took off the sister tug. The *Knot So Fast* had been confiscated by the Crown and put up for auction. Refusing to name names, his uncle was handed maximum, the kind of shit Eddie wanted to avoid. No way he could do that kind of time, stuck in a grimy cell through a coke crash.

The same task-force cops came with their warrant and searched the *Mañana*, turning up nothing. Lucky that time, but it kept Eddie looking over his shoulder. Ramon chalked up Eddie's chickenshit nerves to the poison he was sucking up his nose. Ramon warning him it was fucking him up. Eddie saying he had it under control, no way he was ending up like DeJesus.

"Worse things than doing time," Ramon told him, coming to the bow, handing Eddie a jacket. "Like growing old with nothing to show, no one to grow old with."

Eddie slipped into the jacket, imagined trying to score in prison, thinking what could be worse.

Like he read his mind, Ramon said, "Shit you can get on the outside, you can get on the inside, mostly cheaper."

"Yeah, but what do you do for cash?"

"What you have to," Ramon said. "But to do it, you got to have your head on right. And you, *sobrino*, don't have it on right."

Eddie looked out across the bow, Ramon walking back to the wheelhouse. Eddie thinking his uncle was all pissy on account he got elected to tell the cartel guys on the sub the three hundred Chinese AKs weren't on board, still on a cargo ship caught in a storm, North Korean–flagged. Not his fault, but still . . .

The deal was the coke was coming north, and the AKs were heading south, money changing hands by wire transfer. The sub was making the drop and turning right around. The storm at sea would delay it an extra day, maybe two. Meant the sub needed to hover around in Canadian waters. Not something the cartel bosses would want to hear.

Nothing to do with Eddie; this run paid ten Gs, twenty-five hundred going straight into his pocket. Ten times what dragging logs and busting his hump fetched. For Ramon, it meant smoking better than the native illegals he kept lighting up, his lungs rusting out faster than the old tug.

Coming back from the wheelhouse, his pack of smokes in hand, Ramon tossed a match over the side. Dragging on a fresh one, he let his eyes scan the waters. Looking at Eddie, saying he was full of shit about what he said before. "About all of us having a natural twin."

"What I saw on the *60 Minutes*." Eddie sniffed, saying, "That Morley guy talking about it."

"Fuck him."

"What the man was saying is we all got different DNA, but still, we got a mirror twin. Out there somewhere."

"Guy looks just like me, lights up when I do, pisses when I piss?" Ramon shaking his head, thinking the kid had fried his brain.

"No. Guy pisses when he pisses. Only looks like you. Somewhere out there — in the wide world," Eddie said, no idea why he'd told Ramon in the first place. Wishing he hadn't.

"Don't go believing all the crap on TV, kid," Ramon said, sounding pissy again, dragging on the smoke. "Kind of crap that ups their ratings, doesn't matter if it's true."

"You say so." Eddie hated when Ramon called him kid, his hand twitching on the rail. The zip bag in his pocket.

"Guy doing what I do," Ramon shook his head, dredging up phlegm, leaning and spitting, a herring gull dropping its splatter near the spot, Ramon watching the bird fly off.

"Sure this is the bay, huh?" Eddie asked, putting his twitching hand on the rail.

"Only one deep enough." Shielding his eyes with his hand, Ramon searched around. No cottages. No homes. He thumbed for Eddie to climb up top.

Clomping up the bridge ladder, Eddie leaned over the rail, the rain building up by Hermit.

Ducking into the cabin, Ramon grabbed a soda from the mini-fridge. Cold enough, he popped the top and took a slug, thinking some guy somewhere was doing the same, feeling fizzy pop going down, making his eyes water. Going back out, he called up, "You want one?"

Eddie told him no, turning his head. Nearly jumped, he wagged his hand, pointing.

Looking to the stern, Ramon caught the periscope sawing the surface, a conning tower rising up, water pouring off its hull. Looking like a surfacing whale.

"Jesus H. Christ." Eddie with images of German U-boats. Grabbing the rails, he jumped down, him and Ramon at the port side, the sub pulling alongside. No identifying marking.

Seventy-four feet of Kevlar and carbon fiber, its hull painted a dull camo blue. Colombian coke packed in a Mexi sub surfacing in Canadian waters. Nearly impossible to detect, camouflaged from the air, electric motors running them silent for eighteen hours, twin diesels capable of making ten knots on the surface — high-tech and cutting edge — hugging two thousand kilometers of coastline.

The Baja Maritano cartel was stepping up their game, branching out. Come a long way from extortion on local melon pickers, elbowing into the drug trade, shooting it up with their cartel neighbors and feds on two sides of a border, taking on all comers. Gaining respect.

Cutting a deal with the Santacruz family in Colombia, the Baja Maritanos paid up front for the fleet of subs to be built in the mangroves, hidden deep in an Amazon jungle, the Maritanos ordering up a half dozen more. Two million a pop, pocket change in the drug game.

"Goddamn," Eddie said, watching the hatch flip open.

Thirty years of long-lining salmon and trawling prawn, hauling barges and shoving logs, Ramon looked on. Never seen anything like this. Lighting a fresh smoke, he watched the skinny guy climb out, buzzed hair and a goatee, tattoos on his neck. The guy shielded his eyes, looking over at them, a metal case in his hand, a pistol stuck in his rope belt.

Ramon wagged a hand, not getting a good feeling.

. . . HEAVY BLOW

LINES WERE tossed and tied, the yayo sub bumping the tug's fenders. The stench wafting from the hatch made Eddie turn away, putting fingers over his nose. Smelled like these guys had been pickled in shit and sweat. Nearly a dozen days below the surface with hardly room to turn around. Chowing on what a stray dog would pass up, guzzling *agua* and Leche Gloria, Peruvian condensed milk. A bucket with a makeshift lid for a toilet. Exhaust from the twin diesels seeping in.

Better than a ton and a half of coke crammed the cargo hold, every available space — twenty-seven million bucks for the cartel bosses — these guys with barely room to crawl. A wheel, GPS, radio periscope. Diesel tanks and battery banks packed under the berths.

A ghost slipping undetected past the coast guards of three nations. No choppers, patrol planes, no radar picked them up. Come a long way from the early DIY subs built in the rainforests a decade ago, only capable of short hops from Colombia to Ecuador, easy to spot and unable to dive, sitting ducks with hulls looking like Play-Doh. Most ended up scuttled after delivery, if they made the trip at all. This one was the Cadillac of yayo subs, set to head back with a load of Chinese AKs, the cartel hungry for firepower to take out the judges, officials, politicians, anybody getting in the way of doing business.

Two of the crew hauled up the body, arms limp and hanging to the sides, flesh turned pasty, one guy lifting from under the arms, the other shoving the legs, flopped the body out on the hull. First thought, it was a mannequin. First time Eddie ever saw a corpse. He thought he might puke. Really needed to do that line.

The last of the crew clanged up the steps into daylight, four guys standing atop the hull, squinting and looking around. Unshaven, scrawny, filthy clothes hanging off them, all sucking in Canadian air. Two had tats from head to toe, standing barefoot and shirtless.

All four dove off, trying to rid themselves of the smell, splashing around in the cove, climbing back out. Eddie thinking of the time his Lab got nailed by the skunk under the shed steps, a couple buckets of tomato juice and a week out in the doghouse took care of it. This was worse. Wishing the breeze was going the other way, he kept his hand over his nose.

"The smell of money, kid," Ramon said, walking past and fetching a six-pack of Steam Whistle from inside the cabin door, stepping to the rail, swinging and tossing it, the guy with the goatee catching it. Ramon guessing it didn't matter that the beer was warm, Ramon getting set to tell these guys he didn't have their guns.

Catching the pack against the grubby undershirt, Diego Carrillo Guzmán tore into it and passed the cans around. Popping the top, foam fizzing out, he drank in long swallows, belching, didn't matter it dripped down his chin. Tattoos on his neck looked like vines of barbwire. Goatee trimmed short, hair shorn close to the scalp. The look of a guy in charge, the metal case at his feet, his pistol poking from his rope belt. Popping a second can, he took his time with this one. Tossing the last one to the nearest man, he dropped the empty, torn pack on the deck of the tug, Ramon looking at it, puffing smoke, flicking the butt in the water.

Amado Ramírez Garza caught the last can. A Sinaloan, all sinew and bone, a Little Richard do with bushy brows over deep-set eyes. The two hanging back were Honduran, their bodies covered in tats, every square inch inked, Spanish words and images. The dead guy was Colombian, an out-of-work fisherman named Carlos, crewing on his first run, looking for something better.

Snapping orders in Spanish, Diego waited. The Honduran called Ismael giving him attitude, swallowing his beer, tossing the can onto the tug, tin bouncing around the bow. Took his time and climbed back down the hatch. The other one with ink was Reyes, waiting at the top.

"Couldn't pay me enough go down that hole," Eddie said, fingers over his nose.

"Yeah, I could, kid," Ramon said. "And I were you, I'd keep that shit to myself." Eyes on the Mexican with the pistol, the metal case at his feet, Ramon lit a fresh smoke, fanning out the match. He stepped forward, putting on the friendly, introducing himself and Eddie, saying to Diego, "Supposed to tell you there's a slight delay, amigo. Understand, I'm just passing a message from the guys I work for."

Diego stared, the crew forming a chain, Ismael relaying the

bales from the hatch, legs straddled over the dead man, Reyes passing to Amado. On the bow of the tug, Eddie took the bales and stacked them inside the wheelhouse, setting them anywhere he found space, against the fridge, blocking the hatchway, not enough compartments to hide half of it. Like cocaine heaven. Stacking it by the door, Eddie was drenched in sweat, heart pounding.

Ramon finished explaining, Diego not happy with what he was being told. How they'd have to hide the sub, the crew waiting overnight. The cargo ship coming out of North Korea with the guns got held up by a bad storm, Sea of Japan. Be a day or so before the Rockers from the East Van chapter could get their hands on it, bring it to the sub. Diego thinking he'd have to make the call to Lieutenant Topo Quintero and explain it, not something he wanted to do.

Far as Eddie had been told, they were to run the shit to the North Shore shipyards, dock the tug and truck the load out to Rudi Busch's hunt lodge. Pick up their ten grand. Didn't know anything about three hundred Chinese guns supposed to change hands. Ramon only telling him half of it.

Now Ramon was telling Diego this was a safe spot to hide the sub, extending an invitation for him and his crew, experience some of Rudi Busch's hospitality out at the lodge. Diego's nostrils flared, eyes burning into Ramon, Ramon reminding him he was just the messenger.

Rudi Busch's eldest son was to run a load up to Pemberton. The two bikers back at the lodge waited to pack up Regular Joe's truck and run it overland, a snaking trail through provincial and national parks. Get it to their Spokane brothers. Everybody making serious cash.

Diego put up a hand, Reyes and Amado stopped, each holding a bale. Said he was holding the rest of the coke, about six hundred pounds to stay on board till the East Van chapter made good on the AKs. Ramon argued they'd already been paid. Diego saying, "The way it is." Patting his sidearm. Ramon shrugging, thinking fuck it, he was just the messenger.

Ismael stepped over the dead Colombian, bitching at Diego in Spanish, the two of them getting into it, Diego with his hand on the pistol.

"Is how it is," Diego barked, staring at the Honduran, then back at Ramon, eyeing his surroundings like he was expecting something to jump out.

Ismael spat, turning with the bale, telling the other Honduran to put it back below, Diego calling after him, telling Ismael he was to stay on board and guard it, him and the others checking out this hospitality, saying it in English so Ramon and Eddie understood who was in charge.

Stacking the bale on top of the others by the wheelhouse door, Eddie stepped from the cabin, the first to see it. A charter boat nosed around the bend in the cove, one out-rigger sticking out the side. First thought: marine patrol. Eddie ready to dive over the side, swim for shore. Second thought, it was the East Van bikers here ahead of schedule with the guns. Then as the boat drifted to port, he saw the couple in silhouette, naked bodies on the bridge making out, oblivious to what was going on just off their bow, the guy with his pants at his ankles, his ass pumping, looked like two halves of a melon, the girl pressed against the console, nice tits from what Eddie could tell, bleached bangs in her face, getting vocal about it, slapping his ass like she wanted more of what he was pushing.

Ramon turned and saw the boat, Diego drawing his pistol. All eyes on the couple, *Triggerfish* painted in red along the hull, a cartoon fish and *Coho-a-go-go.com* under the name.

. . . ANY NAKED EYE

BECK EASED her back, reaching for his roll-ups, pulling them up, making sense of things.

"That was it?" Facing him, Vicki couldn't believe it, the guy didn't even break a sweat. Turned in the direction he was looking and now saw the tug. Didn't register what was going on. Men were staring at her. Guys with tattoos. Nothing friendly about any of them. "What the fuck, Beck?" Crossing her arms across her chest, looking for her thong. "Beck?"

"Guess this spot's taken." Cop eyes assessing, Beck did the top button of his pants, nudging Vicki to the side and taking the wheel. He put it together: dope changing hands, an unmarked sub in Canadian waters, the crew loading it onto the tug. Stacks of the shit against the cabin door, saw the guy with the goatee draw the pistol.

"'A quiet cove,' you said." Vicki was using her hands to cover up, ducking behind the console, snatching the tube top off the aft seat, snagging her shorty shorts with her toes, passing to her hand. Hurrying into her clothes, she forgot the thong, the mood shot to hell. A bunch of perverts staring at her. The dead body splayed on top of the sub was lost on her, looked like a guy had too much to drink.

"Get below deck," Beck said, Vicki ignoring him.

Working the EZ Steer, he cranked the trolling motor, set it to reverse, hitting the switch, tilting down the twin Yamahas, aiming to back the hell out of there. Switching the key, all he got was a click. The twin two-fifties giving him nothing. Watching the guy with the pistol, he tried again. Again, nothing.

"Beck?" She straightened her clothes, put on her shoes, finger-combed her hair.

"Won't start." He checked his gauges, tried again.

"You're kidding, right?" Now she was getting pissed, stepping into the open, rain coming down, hands at her hips, calling to the guys gawking, "Hey ya, fellas. Why not take a picture? Last you longer." Putting her shoulders back, all those eyes on her, strange men with tattoos, one of them holding a pistol at his side, Vicki saying, "Jesus, Beck. Can we go?"

"Would if Griff charged the auxiliaries."

"What's that mean?"

"Means we been draining the juice off the cranking batteries."

"And?"

"Not enough left to crank her up." Keeping watch on the men, Beck worked the small Johnson, backing them for the bend, the breeze pushing at his stern, angling them for the rocks. Not the best spot for making a three-point turn with a trolling motor, but it was his only play.

The one with the pistol said something and the guys on the tug started moving, the younger one going to the bow, clanking up its anchor, the older one squeezing past the bales into the wheelhouse, powering up the diesel, water frothing from the props. The one with the pistol jumped from the sub to the tug, coming aft, taking aim at Beck.

One of the tattooed guys slipped into the water and started doing a crawl, rain making rings on the surface. The tug closed the distance, backing low and heavy in the water, Beck guessing they were going to ram him, the young guy coming to the stern with a boat hook.

A few more seconds and he'd be bucked against the rocks. Shifting to neutral, Beck reached in the compartment, pulling his Olin flare from its box. Wasn't exactly his service Glock with a clip of .40 cal, but it was handier and might do the trick.

Watching him shove a shell into the big orange gun, Vicki thinking what the fuck, the thing looking like it belonged on the gun range of Sesame Street — expecting a little sign to pop out of the barrel. *Bang!*

Pressing Vicki into the aft seat, Beck told her sit still and went to the starboard rail, letting the guys on the tug get a look at it, the barrel aimed at the bales. Couldn't miss from that range. The guy with the pistol hesitated, the one in the water still swimming forward.

"No need for that," Ramon threw his throttle to neutral and stepped out and walked to the stern, calling to Beck, tipped up Diego's arm, spoiling his aim, then told Eddie to back off with the hook.

"Gimme some space or we see if your shit's flammable." Beck kept his aim on the bales.

The bales blocked the wheelhouse door. Couldn't shut it. Nothing Ramon could do.

"Okay, amigo, okay," Ramon said, hands held out, twenty feet between the boat and the tug.

Diego raised the pistol back up, knowing he had an easy shot.

"Your buddy puts it away, or we got ourselves a weenie roast," Beck said, finger on the trigger, counting to three.

Ramon slapped Diego's arm. Hard. "Put it away. Can see the man needs his space."

Diego snarled, but tucked it in his rope belt.

"And him, too," Beck nodded at the one in the water, the guy reaching for his transom, blade between his teeth.

Diego barked more Spanish, and Reyes pushed off the transom, paddling back to the sub. Diego kept his glare on Ramon, not liking the way he'd been handled.

Ignoring the look, Ramon told Eddie to take the controls, Eddie doing it, working the engine, thinking Ramon's .357 AMT Backup was within reach. Little gun that made a big hole. Not sure if he'd shoot at the guy on the boat or the freaky Mexican with the pistol.

"Whatever you boys are into's got jack to do with us," Beck called, working the Johnson, backing *Triggerfish* for the mouth of the cove.

"Not what it looks like anyway," Ramon called back, watching the Grady-White backing up.

His English wasn't much, but Diego wondered what the fuck else could it look like? Bales of yayo in plain view, the conning tower of a sub sticking out, the crew standing on its hull, a dead guy splayed like a starfish, Reyes pulling himself up on the gunwale.

"You fellows have a nice day," Beck called, backing away, tucking the flare gun away.

Stepping closer to Ramon, Diego said, "*Puto*'s getting away."

"I can see that."

Back home, Diego would have shot Ramon, shot the naked guy, then shot the woman. Kill them all.

"My job's to move this shit, from here to the shipyard, shipyard to the lodge. Deliver a message about your guns. That's it," Ramon said. "Sure ain't getting mixed up in you shooting people."

"You are stupid, man," Diego said, watching the white boat back around the bend.

"Be more stupid if we don't get the fuck out of here," Ramon said. "Guy gets on his ship-to-shore . . ." Letting that sink in, letting the Mexican figure out the rest.

Cursing, Diego was faced with a delay on the guns, having to hide the sub, staying the night. Everything was going wrong. And he'd only been in Canada about an hour.

"We drive to this lodge." Diego said it like it was his idea. "Eat. Drink. Women."

"First we find someplace to ditch your ride," Ramon said, wondering where the fuck else do you hide seventy-four feet of sub? Squeezing past the bales into his wheelhouse, he switched on the overhead lights, told Eddie to grab his charts. Diego right behind him.

There was a spot off the bottom end of Gambier, secluded enough, double-checking the chart. Making sure it was deep enough, Ramon saying they better get her out in open water, then wait till dusk.

Diego was barking at his men, Ramon tapping a compartment open, taking out his AMT Backup. Not a good time to be unarmed.

Watching Ramon stick the gun in his pocket, Eddie said he was going to the head, feeling the zip bag with the coke in his pocket, going and closing the door, sliding on the lock.

. . . EASY'S GETTING HARD

THE TWO boats bobbed, stern to bow, rope tied to cleats. The old guy from C-Tow had his hand out, palm held flat, expecting Beck to shell out five bills. Said it with a straight face. His name tag said he was Benny, his cap with the earflaps, a beard as coarse as a grill brush, a fleshy nose glowing. Beck pegged him for a boozer, Benny saying he preferred cash.

Digging his wallet from his roll-ups, Beck made a crack about having to pay up front, taking out his plastic, repeating the amount, asking Benny if he was for real.

The C-Tow man said, "Ain't no joking matter out here. All about life and death. You stranded boaters always forgetting that once I tow you in." He sniffed, running his sleeve under his nose, looking at the plastic Beck held out, making no move to take it, saying, "Saving you from one, delivering you to the other. Out here cash is king, my friend."

Benny's breath was a mix of garlic and gin, Beck fishing in his pocket for his roll, saying, "This is what I got." Counting out nearly three hundred in bills, saying, "Day didn't exactly go like I planned."

Benny took his plastic, saying, "But I got to charge you five-fifty."

"How's that?"

"Fees and taxes and so forth." More sniffing. The VISA in his hand, Benny said it was company policy, nothing he could do about it, then went to unearth his credit-card swiper, a wave rocking them. Beck standing on his bow, his foot keeping the boats from knocking.

"Used to be a cop," Beck called after him.

"Me too, long time back, called ourselves Mounties, back when you were sucking on your momma."

Coming back, Benny showed a gap between his front teeth when he grinned. "Badge doesn't mean shit out here, does it, son?" He pointed a black fingernail and showed Beck where to sign.

"Maybe you know a guy, name's Hanson, on the marine patrol," Beck said, taking the swiper, then the pen.

Still grinning, Benny was shaking his head.

"Guy I can call anytime, tell him some ex-cop's out here shaking down disabled boaters." Beck could call Hanson up, but not for favors, the two of them hating each other since the academy.

"Knock yourself out." Benny coughed into his hand, pointed again to where to sign, asking, "What do you got, like four batteries on this girl, son?"

"I going to have to shoot you, Benny?" Beck scribbled to get the ink flowing, signed and handed it back, looking at the gap between the yellow teeth.

"Ought to be thanking me," Benny said, having to leave *Celebrity Boxing*, coming out, braving the chop and finding the Grady-White adrift, its puny trolling Johnson no match for the Strait of Georgia. Nearly past Lighthouse Park, doing a back-and-forth sweep with his mounted search-light, Benny spotted the disabled boat and tossed Beck a line, tied up to his cleat, having to tow them across the inlet in the frigid cold. "Without me, you'd a been screwed, boy. Think you know it." Benny looking at the girl, Vicki sulking and shivering in her life vest, one of those foil rescue blankets around her shoulders, the thing wafer thin. High-heeled shoes on a boat, naked toes exposed. First time he'd seen that.

Two hours past frozen, Vicki's teeth clattered together. The two of them adrift in the dark long after leaving the bay with those creeps, bobbing in the Strait till Beck finally gave up on his trolling motor, calling for a tow, pride keeping him from doing it sooner.

Pissed enough to push him overboard, Vicki put up with Beck making light of it, the guy playing like a tour guide getting towed in, pointing out Stanley Park, over there Jericho Beach, the Burrard Street Bridge, bitching about having to pay the C-Tow guy. Vicki thinking Benny should have charged him double.

Beck had downed the bottle of Johnnie Red like it was antifreeze, this guy that used to be a cop. Four batteries and not enough sense to charge them, blaming somebody named Griff, probably an imaginary friend.

Dropping the fenders, Beck nosed *Triggerfish* into its slip, Burrard Civic Marina, bumping the bow against the dock. No point trying to revive the mood, Vicki barely saying a word to him, sitting on the livewell with her arms folded, wrapped in the stupid rescue blanket.

Beck watched her, knowing this was over, wondering why Griff couldn't get one fucking thing right. Man, you come off a charter, you go through the list: hit the bilge, check the lines for kinks, sharpen hooks, bag the cans and bottles, swab away any puke, wipe down the reels, back off the drags and check the fuel. AND HOOK UP TO SHORE POWER. Simple. A fucking chimp could do it.

Watching her flip off the rescue blanket, Benny pulled away from the dock in *C-Tow 1*. She stepped onto the dock, tossing the vest at Beck's feet. Hugging herself in the denim over the tube-top, she stalked down the dock, heading for the parking lot, didn't give a shit her heels might catch between the dock boards.

"You want, I can give you a lift, or call you a cab?"

"Go hook up your batteries, Beck," she called back to him and kept walking.

Be the only thing he'd be hooking up tonight — watching her pass under the dock lights, those shorty shorts, heels clicking on the wood, the girl not looking back. Not the way the evening was supposed to go. Been looking forward to it all week. Nice-looking girl he met at a Gastown pub. Invited her out for a cruise, calling the fishing charter a yacht. Playing it up. Got a haircut, debating between silk briefs or commando, a bottle of red or a bottle of white, ribbed or scented. Right down to the details: prawns to start, olives with the pimentos, a nice smelly cheese, the salmon fillet, and amaretto for after. He remembered from the pub, the vodka coolers she drank were lime. A four-pack for her, a bottle of Johnnie Red for him, and they were all set.

Beck had Griff take yesterday's charter out solo, Beck doing the running around. Had no idea the girl was vegan — never met one before — still, it would have worked out, the dope runners and flat batteries putting a damper on things. Beck without enough juice to get back home.

Checking his watch, he looked over at Hattie's boat. All dark. Taking his cell, he tapped in her number, damned thing going straight to voicemail. Hanging up, he turned and did an arm whirl, nearly tripping on the empty scotch bottle, sending it spinning. Punching in another number, he bent for the thong on the deck under his chair, felt it between his fingers, remembering she called the color raspberry. Tucking it in a pocket, he waited as the phone rang.

There was a click, Griff sounding sleepy, answering, "Hello?"

Beck saying, "Hey, Griff, buddy, I get you up?"

. . . BODY ENGLISH

NEARLY NINE months since she stuck the knife in the cop. The moaning of sirens forced Ashika Shakira to run that night, leaving the shipment of AKs they were stealing from an Asian gang, using the Jesus Factory as a stash. Guns for the cause. Flutie Al-Nabi had already run off, the one called Baldie Jones lying with a bullet in him.

The Ford had been a late model. She stole it from out front of a Shell station on Main, just blocks from the scene, sirens in the distance, the owner gone looking for the key to the toilet, leaving his own in the ignition. Driving the Kingsway, she found her way to the burbs. Ditching the Ford past Aldergrove, she walked a couple miles of Zero Avenue in the pitch, cutting across farm fields smelling of cow shit, sleeping and shivering in a patch of woods till dawn. Jumping the border, she made it to Lynden.

With no Yankee cash, she played on sympathies, the express bus driver letting her off in Bellingham. Pickpocketed some geezer that looked like he had money, yielded enough cash for a two-bit room and a wig. Snipping her hair in front of the motel mirror, she watched it fall into the sink. Never cared much about what she looked like, Ashika touched the tufts. Setting the scissors down, she put on the wig cap and the Revlon wig colored cinnamon, making adjustments, thinking it looked natural. Looking like somebody else. The name came to her then, Camilla Evangeline Lucci. She said it, rolling it off her tongue until it sounded like she owned it a lifetime, said it till she felt more Camilla than Ashika.

She forced herself to turn a couple of tricks, perched herself at a bar called the Fairhaven, didn't wait long, doing what she had to do, getting her through the week. Money for food, money for the room. Convincing herself the first one wasn't so bad, a businessman with a belly and a Volvo, over before it began in the back seat, the guy apologetic about it. The fat trucker she picked up outside an Arby's paid for a room, bitched about the carpet not matching the drapes, breathed something that smelled like hummus in her face till he came, letting his weight drop on her, Ashika thinking how easy it would be to stick her blade in his neck, getting out from under him, leaving the room with the cash, doing what she had to do.

Money from the tricks got her a change of wardrobe, Ashika tugging up the skinny jeans, snapping on the push-up bra, the faux-leather blouse, the ankle boots, Burberrys marked down, Black Cat shades she got at Chico's — Bellis Fair taking her cash.

Transformed, she checked the mirror on the back of the Holiday Inn bathroom door, not looking like Ashika any-more, the girl who ran the guns, planned the attack on Via Rail, shot Wing Lee, the middleman wearing a wire under his shirt, not the Ashika who stabbed the cop through his flak vest, watching his eyes as the blade went in. Betting there was a Canada-wide warrant for her arrest. Likely made the FBI list, too.

She had read about it a couple of days later, the *Seattle Times* putting a name to the cop she stabbed: Rene Beckman, in stable condition, going to pull through. Ashika was branded a terrorist, the paper showing her likeness, not mentioning Baldie Jones took a cop bullet in the back while his hands were cuffed. It didn't mention Flutie at all.

Three weeks and a couple more tricks kept her in Boomers and coffee, moving to a cheaper room at the Mayflower. Given her choices, she gambled her life and made the call from a pay phone.

The voice on the other end was familiar, with no sound of surprise, the man saying he was glad to hear from her. Like nothing had happened. Like they were old friends. She gave her location, thinking better dead than going to bed with strangers and having to pretend she liked it, impossible to shower them away. It turned out the New Freedom Army still had use for her.

Ashika thought about it now, eight months gone by, looking at her reflection, sliding the tube over her lips, rolling her tongue over the sticky wax, spritzing the Givenchy, stepping through the mist. She picked the new passport off the dresser, flipping it open. *We the people* printed on the inside, the image of the eagle. Camilla Evangeline Lucci. Born in Morocco, 1970. Gave the date of issue, date of expiration, stamped by the Department of State. Looked convincing.

Kim Pang was an artist, forged documents for the New Freedom Army for the better part of a decade, the third set he made for her, put a rush on this one, shipped it UPS, tossing in a birth certificate and driver's license, good enough to pass any cursory inspection.

She slipped it in the handbag with the Bersa .380 Lite, touched a hand to the wig, the tight clothes pinching her. Walking from the chair to the mirror, still getting used to the heels, she was thinking of Flutie Al-Nabi again, jumping off the loading dock that night. Running off. No idea where he ended up. Flutie had hired Baldie Jones to drive, the one Beckman cuffed, the one his rookie partner shot dead on the loading dock. The headlines called it a gun smuggling ring taken down, a victory for the Vancouver cops, making heroes out of Rene Beckman and Danny Green. The cop survived his knife wound, IDed her, sending Ashika to the top of the wanted list: attempted murder of a peace officer, running restricted weapons, part of an international ring, the RCMP tying her to the Via Rail attack back east.

Nothing but dumb luck on their part, bad luck on hers, the two cops rolling by in their patrol car. The photo in the paper showed Rene Beckman in his dress blues, same eyes that had stared into hers, their faces as close as lovers' as she drove the knife through the Kevlar weave. Decorated instead of dead. Now retired from the force. The rookie getting a citation for putting a bullet in Baldie.

The anti-terrorist squad and CSIS would be hunting her, trading info across borders. Bounty hunters would come looking, jackals out for a quick reward. There could be a hit ordered by her own people, a way to minimize their exposure. A bullet in her ear would clean up the mess, remove the risk. But she gambled and went to the pickup point, the Bersa in her pocket, and picked up the wired money. The next call, the voice on the phone told her what to do. Switching to the Motel 6, she lay low and waited, slept with the Bersa, one in the chamber with the safety off. A week passed and nobody came to kill her, Ashika guessing she was still useful. Then came the months of waiting.

Living on pizza specials and egg rolls, Kaopectate kept her regular, daytime soaps kept her from crawling the walls.

Next time the prepaid rang, the voice told her to pick up a key to a flat over a laundromat, other side of town, sit tight and order in. They were moving her around.

Picking up a supply of laxatives, she got the key, the laundromat with an out-of-business sign over the door. Bersa clutched down along her leg, she climbed the stairs, sticking the key in the lock, standing to the side and opening the door. Flicking on a light, she stepped into the near-empty flat. A chair, an old TV and a sagging mattress in one corner, cockroaches scattering like thieves.

Days dragged into weeks, Ashika keeping the Bersa close with the only chair wedged under the door knob, getting into *The Bold and the Beautiful*, getting to know Brooke and Eric and Ridge. Mythos was the takeout place down the block, sent over Greek in tinfoil trays that wasn't half bad. The kid making the deliveries was Tito, told her to try the lamb souvlaki and phyllo pie. Tito earning his tips bringing her the daily papers. She started to tune in to *One Life to Live*, getting to know the Lord family by the time the next call came.

Packing up the suitcase she bought from the Salvation Army store, the one with the telescopic handle, she picked up the silver Accord at the Avis like she was told, taking the route marked on the map in the glovebox, *Art's Grill* and *8* AM written in the margin, the location circled in red. A bundle of twenties next to the map. The voice on the phone didn't say what was up, but she knew by the way they were starting to move her around after eight months of sitting idle that something was in the wind.

. . . BACKWARDS FROM A FORWARD POINT

"SEE, WHAT you're talking about's a psychic," Hattie Winters said, thinking what Beck really needed was a shrink. Across the dock, he stood on his deck. Sometimes he amused her, talking with that stand-up timing. A good-looking guy with more than his share of baggage.

Adjusting the Tilley over hair that needed a wash, longer but her natural shade, Hattie matched herself to the bimbo he had on the boat last night, thinking she stood up. Blocking the sun with the brim, she looked over at *Triggerfish*, Beck's crew, Griffin Cramb sitting and spooling fresh line on a Penn reel, his head down, getting set for the day's charter. Griff was stewing on account of the chewing out he got last night, Beck pulling the cold shoulder on him this morning.

"Okay, so I didn't leave a message," Beck called back to Hattie. "Figured you'd see the call display."

"At one in the morning?"

"Could happen. Sometimes you're up for some tea."

"Oh sure. Your date goes to hell, so you call me?"

"Didn't say it went to hell."

"Didn't have to."

"Come on, wasn't like that."

It was exactly like that. Beck was an open book. Three months since walking out of her own marital nightmare, Hattie took to living on the boat, doing the odd charter to pay the slip fees, always had a knack for finding the schools of salmon. A couple hundred square feet of living space and she felt free. Done with Tim, her bailiff husband working rent distress, collecting money for landlords. Okay, Beck was interesting, but she was starting to see the layers to this ex-cop, not sure she wanted to peel them. Could be another Tim under there, Beck at the bottom of a scotch bottle too much of the time, stuck in the lower chakras the rest of the time.

"I saw her, you know?" Hattie said, grinning. "You helping her on board. Her wearing heels — on a boat." Her grin broadened, Griff hiding his own.

"What? Girl's got her own mind."

"A tube top and shorty shorts screaming *come and get it, boys*." Hattie laughing now, last night's small craft warnings guaranteed the poor trashy girl caught her death. Hattie watching from her porthole when *Triggerfish* was towed in, Trashy storming off, Beck calling Hattie on her cell at one in the morning. Hattie ignoring the call, smiling as she drifted off to sleep.

"Always thinking the worst of me," he said.

"So you didn't call because you were . . ."

"No, I just . . ."

"What? Called to ask where the fish are?" She couldn't help the grin. She'd been out-fishing his boat for the past month straight, Beck coming in skunked half the time. Loved rubbing it in.

"Don't need you finding my fish," he said, then looked at Griff, telling the kid to wind the spool tighter. Griff rolling his eyes.

A hundred yards of fresh twenty-pound already on the Penn. Stripping it off, Griff let the bird's nest fall on top of the old line around his sneakers. Still stinging from the broadside he caught from Beck last night, woken from his sleep — one in the morning — Beck ranting about the batteries not being charged. Told Griff the five bills he paid C-Tow were coming out of his pay, Griff telling Hattie over early-morning tea, saying that was it, asking if she needed a mate, Hattie telling him she'd have a word with Beck, try and smooth it out.

Stepping off *First Light*, she crossed the dock, linen capris and sandals, a crisp white top. Taking off the Tilley, she shook out her hair, using her fingers like a comb.

Beck looked at her, saying, "Heading out?"

"Got a couple coming for ten," she said. "Thinking I'd work the bottom of Bowen. You?"

"Finn's been marking at the mouth of the Cap. Might start there, then maybe the slots."

Stripping the reel, Griff set it aside, taking the handful of monofilament and going down to the galley.

"Finn say what's working?" she said, making small talk now.

"Flash-and-Glos mostly, some going with the Mepps. Didn't say what colors," Beck said, trying to read her. "Bottom of Bowen, huh?

"Should ease up on him," she said, nodding toward the galley.

45

Ignoring her, "What've you been dropping over there?"

"Twitchys mostly."

"The squid?"

"Better luck with the feathers, orange and yellow, bouncing them dead slow."

"You spray them? Fool-a-Fish, something like that?"

"Never makes a difference. Just dead slow this time of year. Sometimes I add a trailer," she said, then, "He's a good kid, you know?"

"Finn mixed up some scents, shrimp and herring, tosses it in the prop wash. Get you some if you want."

"Sounds smelly."

"Yeah." Beck guessed she had her own fishing secrets, keeping them to herself. A girl that fished solo, fairly new at it, hitting more than most, keeping from the cluster of charter boats that stayed hooked up by radio. "How about later?"

"What's later?"

"I'm thinking dinner."

"When?"

"How about dinnertime." He smiled. "Got a nice spring fillet in the box. Could toss it on the grill."

"My boat or yours?"

"You pick."

She gave a shrug, not sure it was a good idea.

"Call you after my charter, give you a chance to decide."

"Long as you don't call at one in the morning, maybe I'll answer." Hattie smiled, thinking of him and Trashy adrift in the Strait.

Stepping up from the galley, Griff held a steaming mug,

looked from one to the other. "Anybody else?" meaning the coffee, taking a sip.

Nobody wanted coffee.

"Got some toast on . . ."

"You see we're talking, right, Griff?" Beck said.

Setting the mug down, Griff sat and got back to spooling the reel, thinking he really needed to google a new job, check out craigslist.

"Really need to snap at him?" she said.

Beck checked his watch, said his half-day charter would be showing soon, businessmen up from Tacoma, repeat customers, the kind that drank heavy and tipped heavier. Smelling something, he turned, smoke puffing from the galley. "Jeez, Griff, what the fuck?"

"Shit." Bounding off the seat, Griff knocked his coffee across the deck, the rod falling over. Banging his head going down the steps, he yanked the toaster's cord, tossing it out on the deck, coughing as he came back up, fanning his arms. The smoke alarm below going off.

Lifting the toaster by its cord, Beck dunked it over the side. Griff grabbed a *Georgia Straight* and fanned it into the cabin, shutting the alarm off, Beck shaking out the toaster on the deck. Soggy, burned bread and blackened paper.

Hattie watched the man drown his own toaster, thinking, yeah, a shrink couldn't hurt.

"Sorry," Griff said, then, "Shit. That was yesterday's tip." Looking at the charred bills.

"Put your tip in my toaster?" Beck asked.

"Hid it in there till I could get to the bank. Forgot about it this time." Griff went for a rag, not wanting Beck looking at him, thinking he'd talk to Hattie later, beg her for a job. Coming back, he got on his knees and started wiping, glancing at her, saying, "Sorry for the cursing, Hattie."

"Hope it wasn't a lot," she said.

"Forty bucks."

Excusing herself, she recrossed the dock, stepped over her transom, Beck watching, trying to picture her in heels.

"So much for breakfast," Griff said, scooping up the bits.

Beck checked his watch again, thinking back to why he hired the kid: a former lifeguard, captain of his school swim-team. Didn't expect him to be so damn dumb. Gave him the job in case some drunk fell overboard. The way Beck had been drinking since leaving the force, he figured maybe it would be him.

Beck's phone chirped. Taking it from his windbreaker draped over the chair, he checked the display. Vicki Moon.

Surprised, he stepped along the bow rail to the pulpit, getting out of earshot, answering on the third ring.

"You thawed?"

"Funny guy." Sounding friendly enough. "Lucky frost-bite didn't take a toe."

"Glad it's you calling and not your lawyer."

"Could come after you for hypothermia, that and prom-ises not delivered."

"Could make that part right," he said.

"Guess that's why I'm calling."

"Yeah?" Beck felt his heart shift gears, thinking how how how and boom boom boom.

"Doing anything later?"

"Got a charter till noon. Clear after that." His luck taking a turn.

"How about you meet me downtown?"

"Just name the place."

"West Georgia and Granville. You know where the Bay is?"

"Sure."

"Say two."

"I'm there." Thinking of her raspberry thong, thinking he should hand it back. "What've you got in mind?"

"A little sightseeing, a little dinner after. Nice vegan place I mentioned."

"Yeah, right. Vegan, huh?"

"Gonna love it." And she hung up.

The girl had defrosted after her night out on the Strait, got past thinking it was the worst date of her life. Taking him to dinner. Could be the way he handled the six guys with just his flare, playing it like he still had a badge. Could be about finishing what he and Vicki started.

Okay, he'd tank up the Jeep, check the oil. Leave nothing to chance. Coming around the rail, he looked over at *First Light*, Hattie not on her deck. Griff finished mopping the spill, then tightened the reel on the rod.

Taking a pair of twenties from his wallet, Beck held them out.

"What's that?"

"The tip you lost," Beck said, wagging the bills.

. . . LYING LOW

SEEN HIS share of blow, mostly grams and eighths. But this was something else. Thirty-two bales packed in back of a moving truck, weighing something like fifty pounds apiece, the bikers back at Rudi's saying this shit was uncut, Eddie doing the math, figuring what a single bale could fetch. Hard to believe.

Nearly two in the morning by the time they hid the sub up by Gambier, left the one called Ismael on board with the dead guy and a dozen bales of the coke. The rest of them got back to the shipyards and packed the coke into the back of the rental truck. Diego wanted to head out, get to the lodge, Ramon saying it would look suspicious, a moving truck driving to Hope in the middle of the night.

The five of them spent the rest of the night in the truck, Ramon and Eddie up front, Diego and his boys in back: Reyes and Amado lying on the metal floor, Diego propped against a bale. Fitful sleep for those who could sleep, barely a word between the rest. Dark eyes with thousand-yard stares, all had seen their share of horrific shit back where they came from, living with the ghosts of it. Doing what they had to to survive.

Soon as the sun showed, Ramon got out of the driver's side and went searching for coffee, coming back juggling a tray of takeout cups.

Getting up in back and stretching, Diego drank the coffee, the metal case close to his feet, pistol in his belt. He told Eddie to get behind the wheel.

"I'll drive," Ramon said, keys in one hand, coffee in the other.

"No, him," Diego said, pointing at Eddie.

Ramon shrugged and stuck the keys in the ignition, the two of them switching places. Diego looking at him, still pissed about the guns, not forgetting the way Ramon slapped down his pistol hand. Did it twice.

Ismael stayed on the sub. Diego's orders. Said no to leaving the other Honduran called Reyes, Ismael arguing he couldn't run it alone, in case he had to scuttle her. Diego said that's the way he wanted it, staring back at the man, hand on the pistol. No way he was chancing the two Hondurans taking off in the sub, leaving him stranded.

Diego squatted in the doorway between the cab and cargo, the other two settling back on the floor, drinking coffee. Amado was tall and rangy. The one with the shaved head and gang ink was Reyes, the guy not saying a word to anybody.

Cracking his window, Eddie put her in gear and rolled, went back to doing the math in his head. A gram went for a hundred on the street. Thirty-two bales in back, a dozen more on the sub, hidden at the bottom end of Gambier. The one called Ismael left to guard it, a crazy looking dude, covered head to toe in tats.

"Any idea what this shit goes for?" Eddie said to Ramon.

"Just watch your speed, kid."

"They want to pull me over, then what?"

"Then I teach you how to jail."

Eddie eased up on the pedal, felt the coke lump in his pocket, no chance to do it till they got to Hope, saying, "Regular Joe said something about another run in a month."

"Yeah, Joe talks a lot," Ramon said, knowing the cartel would blame the bikers for the delay on the guns, didn't matter about the storm at sea. Any more fuck-ups and the cartel might send more than a sub crew the next time. These guys not known for their gentle nature. Not something Ramon wanted to get caught in.

Clicking on the AM, Eddie twisted the knob, landed on an old Hoople number, tapping the wheel, still doing the math.

Diego told Eddie to turn that shit off. Amado, with the Little Richard pomp, crabbed his way to the back corner, working down his pants, pissing into his empty Styro cup.

Eddie switched off the radio, looked at Ramon. His uncle leaning back in his seat, said he was going back to thinking about his natural double, then closed his eyes.

Amado came forward, tossing the cup of piss out Eddie's window.

Keeping to the speed limit in the outside lane, his arm out the window, Eddie took them past Abbotsford, Chilliwack and finally Hope, swinging onto the Crowsnest. First thing he was doing when they stopped, he'd go to the can and do the line, Eddie needing a good buzz.

Glancing at the visor's vanity mirror, he kept an eye on the guys in back, Diego with the vibe of that badass from

Sexy Beast, stone-cold eyes framed by caterpillar brows. Had a hard-on for Ramon for slapping his gun hand down. Made the man look bad in front of his crew.

After the naked couple had backed the pleasure boat from the bay, Ramon guided the sub to a deep channel, waited till dark, took them to the new spot, some sunken pilings from an old pier at the bottom end of Centre Bay, Gambier Island. They hauled what cedar boughs and debris they found along the shore in the dark, covering the conning tower, left Ismael sitting at the hatch with the bullpup, a Kel-Tec KSG. Ejected down, not forward, two feet long, weighing under seven pounds, twelve rounds, made in the U.S. of A., promising a light recoil. Right out of its crate, still had that new-gun smell.

Eddie drove the county road, dust stirring under the rubber. He hung a right past a faded wood sign declaring it Busch's lodge, a country mailbox out front, used to be red. A hunt lodge, back in the day, Rudi Busch making a living as an outfitter then, offering guide service to city boys with wallets thick enough to come and play hunter, Rudi escorting their drunken asses to where the bear and deer roamed.

When the bikers started showing up, the fat city boys stopped coming. Rudi gave up on the guiding, running drugs and guns a hell of a lot more lucrative, Rudi trading trophy heads for a cash cow, getting his sons in on the new family trade, the two of them driving Beemers and dressing all *GQ*.

Eddie swung onto the old service road, west side of the lodge, rolling the truck around back, not more than wheel tracks with high grass in the center, a marsh to the left, branches scraping at the box. Eddie pulled up to the spot Rudi's kid Axel motioned to. Eddie looking at this guy his own age, giving orders in three-hundred-dollar jeans, a designer shirt with the sleeves rolled.

Standing by his kitchen door, Rudi Busch watched, had that Vinnie Jones look about him, a guy with a hard bark. Getting out of the cab, Eddie was told to unload the bales, Axel snapping the orders, pointing to the wheelbarrows.

"Got to go to the can," Eddie said.

"That can wait," Axel said, pointing to the barrows.

Eddie saw Rudi Busch watching, did like he was told.

The two bikers stood in the shade behind the lodge, leaning and smoking, no Rockers colors showing. They took in the unloading. Regular Joe was the taller one, thick-boned with old scars showing the kind of life he lived, a beat-to-hell porkpie hat on his head, an Iron Jaw T-shirt under a denim vest that looked like it had been used to mop up motor oil, the sleeves chewed off.

Hair slicked back, Billy Wall had been sergeant at arms of the Spokane chapter since his Golden Gloves days, about three belt notches ago. The words *Pain is temporary* ran up one big forearm, *Pride is forever* down the other.

Diego and Amado walked over to Rudi, Ramon making the introductions, Rudi telling him to go help his nephew unload, doing the talking, looking at Diego, making promises about the guns.

Setting a bale on top of a couple more, Eddie rolled the barrow over to the last cabin, careful not to let it tip, Axel Busch pointing to a spot. He told Eddie that was far enough.

Taking it from there, Axel wheeled the barrow around back of the end cabin, along a thin trail into the woods.

Stepping over, Billy Wall asked Eddie what he thought he was doing, Ramon coming with the second barrow, setting it down. Billy motioned them back to the truck, told them to wait there for the barrows. They walked over, Eddie taking in the row of cabins out back of the lodge, six of them, one the same as the next, board-and-batten siding with a tin roof, a river-rock chimney, looked like what the Clampetts lived in before they struck oil.

Axel came back with the empty barrow, set it down, asked Eddie what he was waiting for, told him to fetch another load, Eddie saying the next load was going to be the one in his pants, saying he had to go to the can, Axel telling him that could wait, then he rolled Ramon's barrow around the back. Ramon hooking Eddie's sleeve, telling him to do like he was told. The bikers watching.

. . . THE DEVIL'S BED

THE LAST of the coke was off the truck, everybody filing through the back door, Eddie heading for the can, fishing the zip bag from his stash pocket, the great room done in pine board, a trophy bighorn over the river-rock fireplace at the far end, a couple of armchairs facing it. Moose heads, deer, boar and bear lined the walls. A pair of sofas with wooden arms flanked a pine table; dining tables and chairs were in the center of the room, a billiard table halfway to the bar. Well-stocked shelves, a brass rail and swivel stools, swinging doors leading to the kitchen.

Finding the can, Eddie flipped on the lights and switched the lock, got his VISA from his wallet, tapped the line on the porcelain, took out a bill and rolled it. Sniffed it up, came up — yeah — smiling at the guy in the mirror.

Flushing the toilet, he checked for powder around his nose, then went back past the trophies, stood next to his uncle. Feeling alright.

Ramon looked at him, handed him a dripping beer, put his back to the knotty pine. Rudi and Diego were on opposite sides of the bar, head to head, glasses in front of them, talking business under the Labbatt neon, Rudi not happy about Diego holding back a dozen bales that had been paid for, explaining most of the coke was to be put on the old 4 × 4 out front, the bikers taking it through provincial to national forests, getting it in the hands of the Spokane Rockers at some remote spot, a place called Brewster. Sure didn't want to make the run twice.

Diego shrugged, wanted to know about the guns, no desire to explain the delay to Lieutenant Topo.

Rudi told him the freighter was making its way, all three hundred guns on a container.

Diego saying, "Then everyone has to wait." Knocking back his drink, looking at the bottles lining the shelves behind Rudi.

Rudi said he'd have to make a call to the chapter pres, refilled his own glass, saying, "Meantime, you boys want to get cleaned up?"

"Twelve days with no toilet," Diego said. "What you think, amigo?"

"See, what I'm doing here," Rudi said, leaning close, "is laying out the welcome mat. Not my fault your guns didn't show." He took the bottle and poured more in Diego's glass. "What say you make the best of it?"

Diego downed his drink, slid the glass back, thanking him in Spanish.

"Have my boy fix you fellas something to eat." Rudi poured again. Stepping to the swinging door, he rapped, told Axel to keep their new friends in drink, Reyes and Amado leaning by the cue rack, watching the bikers shoot pool. Going back behind the bar, Rudi said to Diego, "Had the pressure fixed, showers working pretty good now." Sipping his own drink, saying, "Different story a week ago." Rudi thinking the smell rising off this guy beat any stink bait he ever concocted for bagging bear, asking him, "You want a beer to chase that?"

Diego slid his glass again, saying, "American beer is shit."

"Know you're in Canada, right, amigo?" Rudi said, not letting this guy get to him, pouring. "You want to put on the feedbag, let my boy know. We got bologna, go nice with some Vidalia onion, or there's ham and cheese, maybe turkey. Take your pick." Rudi reached across and clapped Diego on the shoulder, putting enough of his two hundred pounds behind it.

"Steak," Diego said, showing Rudi about an inch thick with his thumb and finger, black under his fingernails.

Feeling the buzz, Eddie stood next to his uncle, betting the guy wanted it bloody.

Rudi telling Diego they had a nice spud salad: onion, celery, capers, mayo, pickle. "Girl from town comes in, makes it fresh, puts in Granny Smith apple. Ever have it like that? Go real nice with your sandwich."

Diego saying he wanted to see this girl from town, Rudi picking up the bottle again, refilling the Mexican's glass, saying he wasn't going to be here that long.

Grabbing a case of Canadian, Axel restocked the fridge, lining the shelves. Pissed off at his old man. Told to make sandwiches for these smelly guys, being ordered around in front of everybody, treated like the hired help.

"Anything else you boys need, just got to ask," Rudi said, smiling, putting the bottle down.

"The ones that saw?" Diego said, pushing his glass forward again, then waving Amado over, his eyes finding on Ramon.

"Yeah?" Rudi said, already heard the story about the naked couple on the boat.

"Alive is no good."

"Wouldn't worry about it," Rudi said, taking the bottle again, topping off the Mexican's glass, one more for himself. "Sub's in a good spot. Guns are coming. Best thing's we all keep a low profile."

Diego shook his head, saying, "They see what they cannot see." He reached to the floor and took the metal case and set it on the bar. It was time to make the call, not one he wanted to make.

Rudi watched Diego take the sat phone from the lined case, insert a battery, its GPS and SOS dismantled. Punching in a number, Diego waited, then spoke in Spanish. Sounded like he was catching hell from the other end, barely getting in a word. Then he handed the phone to Rudi, letting Rudi get an earful of broken English, this Lieutenant Topo Quintero on the other end, the guy who ordered up heads on pikes, Rudi trying to keep the peace, keep this deal alive. When Topo finished ranting, Rudi said yeah and handed the phone back.

Diego popped out the battery, put the phone back in the case, looking at Ramon.

"Okay, so we take care of the naked couple," Rudi said, waving the bikers over.

"Him," Diego said, pointing at Eddie.

Eddie feeling like he'd been slapped. Everybody looking at him. Middle of a coke buzz.

"You don't want him," Rudi said, kind of laughing, Eddie looking like he might piss himself.

"*Sí.*"

"Want him to do the guy on the boat?"

"And woman."

"Come on," Ramon said. "Eddie doesn't do wet work."

Diego grabbed for the phone, popped the battery back in.

"Okay." Rudi sighed, wagged a finger, Ramon and Eddie stepping over.

Too high for this. Eddie wanted his legs to start running, looking to Ramon, his uncle nudging him to the bar.

"Going to take the couple out, kid," Rudi said, matter of fact.

Ramon saying to Rudi, "Kid agreed to make the run from the tug to here. That's it."

"On account of the delay," Rudi said, "these guys can't have witnesses."

Chickenshit gringo. Diego grinned at Ramon, saying, "You go with. Help him hold his gun."

"Man on the phone wants it done," Rudi said to Ramon. "Customer's always right. All there is to it."

"Just walk up to some guy —" Eddie started.

Slamming his hand flat, Rudi said, "Man the fuck up, kid."

Diego took the Taurus from his rope belt, Rudi's hand slipping under the bar. Axel stopped loading the beer, the broom closet a few steps away. The twelve gauge next to the mop and bucket, loaded and set to go. Regular Joe and Billy Wall stopped knocking balls around, watching the play at the bar.

Diego slid the piece along the bar, telling Eddie to pick it up.

Eddie didn't move.

Finally, Ramon reached for it. "Fuck it, I got this."

"No," Diego said, hand down on the piece, pointing at Eddie. "Him." Pressing the gun into his hand, Diego closed his fingers around it, saying, "Amado goes with. Sees it is done."

Rudi looked at the Sinaloan with the pomp, then at Ramon, saying, "Shouldn't have pissed him off."

"How it is," Diego said.

Eddie was way too high for this.

Diego slid off the stool and headed for the door marked *Authorized Personnel Only*. Looked at Axel and showed him how thick he wanted his steak, Amado following him out.

Ramon looked at Rudi, saying, "Come on, man. You know he's not right for this, the guy's pissed at me, slapped his gun down. You want it done without a hitch, you send them." Looking at Billy and Regular Joe, saying, "No offense."

"Somebody tell you this was nine-to-five?" Rudi said, looking from Ramon to Eddie. "You show up and punch a clock?"

"Agreed to run your shit," Ramon said. "That's all."

"He does it . . ." Rudi leaned across the bar, looking hard from one to the other.

"Look Rudi —"

Rudi's fist caught Ramon flush on the jaw, bouncing him back off the paneling, Ramon holding the side of his face, staring back.

"Only way out's pray the guns show before you find the couple on the boat." Done talking, Rudi walked by the pool table, past the fireplace, the trophy heads looking down.

Lining his shot, Regular Joe said to Billy Wall, "Guy's got a punch."

"For an old guy," Billy said, waiting for Joe to take his shot.

Joe leaned, pulled the cue back. Reyes finished his can of beer, came off the wall, bumping past him, going for the door, following the Mexicans.

The ball bounced from the pocket, Joe looking at the back of the Honduran, saying, "Fuckin' taking that over."

... BODY LANGUAGE

"Gᴏᴛ ᴛᴏ be shitting me," Beck said, not believing it.

A passerby turned, giving him a look. Beck was staring at Vicki in nothing but a thong and cruel shoes, the corner of West Georgia and Granville. Busy downtown Vancouver, city of a couple million. Broad daylight. Pedestrians stopping and staring, shooting her mixed looks, the women scowling, men bumping into things.

A black thong this time. The cardboard sign in front of her chest said: *Do It Vegan.* Her body painted like a diagram of meat cuts: *LOIN*, *THIGH*, *SHANK*, *RIB*, *CHUCK* and *SHOULDER*. *RU* on one butt cheek, *MP* on the other.

"Jesus," he said, stepping up, the girl begging for the first uniform to drag her off in cuffs, write up misdemeanor charges: indecent exposure, causing a disturbance, disorderly conduct, public indecency, lascivious behavior. "You high or something?"

"Meat. I'm protesting it." Vicki said it matter of fact, passing him a pamphlet. The ʜᴇᴀʀᴛ logo on the front, Humane and Ethical Animal Rights Team. Pics and info graced the spread, a tear-off mailer for donations.

"Thought we were doing dinner?"

"That's later."

A second near-naked girl stood on the corner by the newspaper boxes, marked up the same way, standing in pumps and a thong, hers green. She handed out pamphlets.

A guy with some size leaned against the stone corner of the Bay building, shirt half open, jeans over cowboy boots, looking like their pimp, keeping an eye on the girls.

"Say we get you out of here?" Beck said, guessing somebody slipped something in her drink, maybe the pimp.

"Not till I finish my shift." Then she laughed. "You should see your face." Vicki handing a pamphlet to a passerby.

Told him on the boat she volunteered for HEART from time to time. Beck had figured she typed letters, took calls from behind a desk. Could picture some judge handing down psychiatric tests, have her checked out for crossed wires, make her pee in a cup.

"Got to do it naked?"

"Technically, I'm not. Thing is, it creates awareness. Speaking out for those who can't." She liked that she shocked him, saying, "Come on, Beck, gave you way more sugar last night." She was enjoying this.

"Yeah, but . . ."

Turning for the corner, she gave him a look at the *RU* and *MP*, handing a silver-hair in pinstripes a pamphlet, the senior taking it, thanking her and walking away, looking over his shoulder.

Last night left him lying awake, listening to the water lap at his hull, *Triggerfish* in its slip at the Burrard Civic Marina, the hum of the batteries charging away. He got in his share of picturing her naked, remembering the way she felt, the guys on the yayo sub and tug spoiling the moment.

More than once he looked out his cabin window over at Hattie's boat, tempted to go tap on her door. Play it cute, say a cup of herbal tea might help him sleep. But Hattie had been watching when he cruised out with Vicki. Seen Vicki in her heels. No point knocking after the phone call, Hattie not picking up. One in the morning.

Now here he was, a second chance with Vicki; it might work out if she didn't get busted first. Passing out pamphlets, she posed for a camera phone, slinging an arm around the other girl, popping her heel up the way models used to do in those cheesecake black-and-whites.

A courier pulled his bike onto the curb, took a pamphlet, asking what he'd get if he read it. She told him "Informed," the guy riding back into traffic, catching the light. Made his day.

Checking out the pimp, the guy looking back at Beck. A wave of pedestrians crossed between them, more coming up the stairs of the SkyTrain station, crossing the street, the girls nearly out of pamphlets. Cell phones snapped pics, people stopping, asking questions, getting informed. Some woman said they ought to be flogged. A group of high-school boys committed body parts to memory. Hormones, got to love them.

A guy stuck his head out his van's window, big beard flowing, threw a kiss, offering ten bucks for the girls to take down their signs.

"Can't, he's a cop." Vicki pointed at Beck, the bearded guy flipping Beck the bird, the van rolling through an amber light.

More poses, more pics, the girls informing the public,

keeping their signs in front of their chests. Sure to rocket off the YouTube charts, go viral on the net. Likely make the six o'clock news. Doing it till they ran out of pamphlets.

The pimp still eyed him, Vicki calling Beck over, introducing him to the other girl, Tori, younger than Vicki, blonde and marked up the same way, getting her share of looks. Tori offered a soft hand, letting the sign slip, teasing him, saying, "You're the fella with the boat, right?"

"Guess I am," Beck said, shaking her hand, not letting his eyes drop.

"Vicki sent me the pics," Tori said, giving his hand a squeeze. "Nice-looking boat by the way." Looking him up and down.

"Thanks, I guess."

Tori said to Vicki, "You're right, he is cute." Letting go of Beck's hand, saying she'd love to hear how he got the scar sometime, turning and going back to informing the public.

The pimp pushed off the wall and stepped over, thumbs in his belt loops, slinging an arm around Vicki, a HEART button on his lapel. Pushing forty, a marine haircut, hairline receding, and a hawk nose. A bit taller than Beck in the cowboy boots. Likely there to protect the girls from the carnivores they were handing pamphlets to, whisk them out of there if the cops pulled up.

"Oh Beck, this is Jimmy," Vicki said.

The pimp stuck out his hand, saying, "You're the dude with the boat."

Beck shook the hand, saying to her, "Anybody you didn't tell?"

"You were on the force, am I right?" Jimmy squeezed.

"Right," Beck said, returning the grip.

"Tough luck, running out of gas." Jimmy grinned, not letting go.

"Gas was fine. Was the batteries that went flat."

"Got to charge those puppies up," Jimmy said, pumping the hand.

"Yeah, thanks."

"And you pointing your big orange gun," Jimmy said, shaking his head. "Wish I'd been there."

Beck took his hand back, asking, "You with HEART, Jimmy?"

"Me, no. Just lending moral support. I'm with an outfit, call ourselves the Sea Rangers."

"Sea Rangers, huh? That come with a badge and whistle?"

Jimmy lost the grin, saying they were into anti-whaling down in the Southern Ocean. Making a difference.

"Like those guys on TV?"

"We help each other out from time to time."

Tori stepped from the corner, out of pamphlets, putting an arm around Jimmy, asking him, "You working on Beck, signing him up?"

"Can always use a good man."

"I'm doing it," Vicki said to Beck.

"What, the Southern Ocean?" Beck said, surprised. "Even colder down there."

"We'll keep her warm, don't you worry," Jimmy said, arms going around both girls, telling them to lift their signs a bit. "Like poker, girls. Got to hold 'em close."

Somebody took a shot of the three of them, Vicki handing out a pamphlet.

"Tough gig being a cop," Jimmy said.

"Not for everybody," Beck said, liking the pimp less every time his mouth moved.

"Did my bit in the military."

"That right?"

"Two tours. Kosovo and Sudan."

Beck bet field-kitchen duty, maybe relocating civilians.

"Got lucky," Jimmy said. "Put me right out there on the front lines."

"Saw action, huh?"

"Some."

"Tour of duty, what's that, six months?"

Jimmy grinned.

A guy in discount tweed interrupted the head-butting, setting his briefcase on one of the paper-boxes, asked Jimmy if he'd mind getting out of the shot, the girls getting in nice and tight, showing smiles behind the signs, the guy snapping away with his cell, saying this was going right up on the mantle, thanked them and went on his way.

"We about done?" Beck asked Vicki.

"Little early to eat, no?" she said.

"Any other surprises?"

"Could play a little Officer Down." Toying with him, she handed out her last pamphlet, a rotund woman with yellow Bay bags taking it — a bit reluctantly.

"She say where we're eating?" Jimmy asked him.

Beck looked at him, then back at Vicki, Rotund waving a sausage finger in her face, telling her she ought to be ashamed. An old gent with a cane stopped and said, "Thought the loin was in the back."

Assuring the guy hers went all the way through, Vicki moved her leg, demonstrating, Beck and Jimmy watching. The guy with the cane thanked her for clearing that up, then was dragged away by Rotund, handing him the yellow bags.

Staring at her, a kid on a longboard rode straight into the *Sun* box, nearly tumbling into the street. A CTV News van screeched to a stop, honking, its bumper just missing the kid.

Pedestrians milled around, the news crew piling out of the van's sliding door, a guy with a green mohawk hoisting a JVC to his shoulder, Beck recognizing the blonde reporter from TV, the woman stepping from the passenger seat, smoothing her outfit, every hair sprayed in place. Interviewed him one time at a crime scene on the Eastside, a vicious bitch with a smile and a microphone.

A squad car pulled up behind the news van, and there was his old partner Danny Green, stepping out of the passenger side, snugging his cap, checking out the disturbance, seeing the girls with the signs, glancing at the gathering crowd, smiling when he saw Beck, shaking his head and stepping over, leaving the scene to his rookie partner.

Danny turned enough to watch the rookie handle things, the young female officer getting out her pad, one hand on her nightstick, asking Vicki and Tori if she could see their permit, Jimmy stepping in to straighten things out, the rookie telling him to step back.

"Last I heard," Danny said, "you got yourself into a charter boat."

"Heard right," Beck said. "Took the afternoon off, came down to meet my date. Going to dinner if your partner doesn't arrest her first."

Danny looked over at the girls. "Yeah? Which one?"

Beck pointed.

"Nice." Danny nodded, Beck guessing he still felt bad for the night Beck was stabbed, blaming himself for his rookie mistake, taking out the nightstick instead of the Glock.

Beck pointed at Danny's partner. "Fresh out of Depot, huh?"

"Yeah, she's coming along, though," Danny said.

"That was you two years back."

They watched Jimmy trying to defuse the situation, Vicki and Tori arguing, Danny's partner warning Jimmy again to step back, hand on her nightstick, same way Danny used to handle things.

"That guy a chaperone or a pimp?" Danny said.

"Arrest him if you want."

Danny started walking, saying he better step in. "Before she takes the stick to him."

"You ever feel like wetting a line . . ." Beck called.

Danny nodded, said for sure, then stepped into the scene, the two girls with their signs, harping about their rights. Danny steered his new partner out of the cameraman's line of fire, the blonde reporter asking why the girls were marked up like meat.

. . . MADMEN ON THE WATER

HE WASN'T sure at first. Could have been the screech of a seabird. The girls had gone off down the passageway, headed for the galley to scrub off the ink, lit up and buzzing over the HEART thing, nearly getting arrested, Jimmy volunteering to help with the scrubbing, told to wait with Beck.

The two of them left in Jimmy's cabin, Jimmy and Beck looking at each other, not saying much. Then Jimmy went off in search of coffee.

On the narrow bunk, Beck looked around the cabin, the engines rumbling below decks, the engineer running his checks and tests, making adjustments. Beck taking everything in: the metal room all grey, no window, no closet. A Greenpeace poster declared, *WE FUCKED UP EARTH*. A beat-up suitcase in one corner, a guitar case against the desk, said *Gibson* on it. Jeans and Ts hung from the door hook. For a guy pushing forty, a Gibson and jeans weren't much to show.

"You play, or it just for show?" Beck asked when Jimmy came back, Jimmy handing him one of the Styro cups. He said the guitar killed the boredom, wasn't a lot of TV to watch in the Antarctic, telling Beck about the ship: fifty-six meters of riveted steel, *RESEARCH* painted down both sides, on the block for two years before the Sea Rangers made their bid. Told him about the board of directors, an ex-chair from some council on international alliance, an activist from the Capital who used to flog sustainable development for Greenpeace, along with an assortment of tree-hugging philanthropists. Jimmy said the man with the captain's cap was ex-navy: Angus Hilton, with the Donald Sutherland looks, a good egg when he wasn't into his cups — why he wasn't still with the navy.

The Sea Ranger cause was shaping into a government nonprofit deal. The aim was to outfit the ship and form a crew, sail her to the Southern Ocean, assist Greenpeace and the Sea Shepherds, see that the Japanese refrained from whaling, assert a Canadian presence, gain international points. Jimmy saying the federal government was playing look-over-there, diverting attention from the other coast, Canadian citizens beating seal pups with clubs, spoiling the America Lite image. The kind of thing that didn't look good in world news.

Jimmy saw himself in the chief officer spot, second-in-command, waiting on the board's vote.

Beck blew at the steaming coffee, sipping it, burning his tongue. Tasted a week old, bitter and reborn from old grounds.

"Need sugar?"

"Need someplace to spit." Beck thinking a shot of whiskey wouldn't save it.

Jimmy pulled packets of sugar and powdered cream from a pocket, said it might help.

"It's fine." Beck set the cup between his shoes.

"The way Angus likes it," Jimmy said. "Guy tosses the powdered stuff in his."

"Stuff circus clowns light on fire."

"Yeah." Parking himself backwards on the chair, Jimmy leaned in, saying, "So, which one?"

"Which one what?"

"Vicki or Tori?"

"We tossing for the girls?"

"Just asking."

"See, Vicki invited me down. Was thinking we were having dinner, as in just the two of us."

"Full of surprises, that one," Jimmy said, shaking his head.

"Yeah." Dinner turning into a group effort, Beck figuring she was getting even for last night. The ship's engines rumbled louder, the Styro cup at Beck's feet showing rings from the vibration. They sat quiet for a while, Jimmy sipping, Beck asking, "You got a target date?"

"Was thinking Tori, but if you —"

"Meant the Southern Ocean, going to save whales."

"Ah, well, soon as we get past the red tape."

Beck nodded.

"Pain in the ass getting a committee to agree on the simplest shit," Jimmy said.

"Tell me about it." Reminded Beck of his days in uniform, red tape and policy change, memos like clockwork.

"Right now they're debating what color to paint the hull, camo gray or leave her white. Going back and forth. Then there's coming up with a name." Jimmy rolling his eyes.

"For the ship?"

"Yeah. Some going for an environmental lean, most wanting a celebrity's name down her sides."

"Yeah, like who?"

"Some going with David Suzuki."

"A name the Japanese would get."

"Right. Captain's on the fence between the SS *Bieber* or the *Bublé*."

"Bieber, the kid singer?"

"The daughter thinks he's cute, wife thinks the other's got talent. Were up to Angus, I think he'd go Pam Anderson."

"Pam, huh?"

"Other names got tossed around: Keanu Reeves, Trebek, that Linkletter guy, Howie Mandel . . . guy that played Doc Hollywood . . ." Jimmy snapped his fingers, couldn't come up with the name. "Hockey goalie, got his teeth knocked out all the time . . ."

"Johnny Bower," Beck said. "Used to call him the China Wall."

"And that guy played Captain Kirk." Jimmy sipped, saying, "Me, I say we go Neil Young. Most talented guy in the country."

"Hard to argue." Beck saying he loved the tune about the chick on the Harley.

"Trouble is, board thinks old Neil throws off a homeless vibe, gives the wrong impression," Jimmy said. "Only way he gets on board is if we pipe his tunes through the PA."

"Taking a film crew?" Beck thinking Vicki would be all over it.

"Had talks with the Cousteau people. Guys from Nickelback practically begging to do the theme track."

Nodding, Beck wondered what was keeping the girls, Jimmy mentioning a wine-and-alternative-cheese do Captain Angus was throwing up in the wheelhouse, drumming up support, saying they could go up for a drink when the girls got back.

"Vegans drink wine, huh?"

"Sure, vegan wine. We got Absolut, Amaretto if you're a chick, Bacardi, Baileys, Chivas, you name it."

"Wash down the Tofurky, huh?"

Jimmy looked thoughtful, then said, "She told me, you know?"

"Told you what?"

"About you two in that bay." He took a sip. "The tug and the guys staring, you pulling your flare gun. Wasn't till later, she got that it was a sub."

"A sub? Come on, Jimmy. This is the other Colombia."

"Showed me the shot she took," Jimmy said, "one with you naked. Sub in the background, a bit soft, but, no doubt what it was."

"Yeah, well . . ."

"Running dope?"

Beck shrugged.

"Ask me, these guys aren't going to leave loose ends."

"They come back, then I do something about it."

"They come, they'll come for her, too," Jimmy said.

"Like I said . . ."

"How about your cop buddies, still got some, right?"

Over the rumble of the engines came the clanking of heels on steel.

Vicki stepped through the doorway in skinny jeans, heels and a T that said *SEA RANGERS CREW*.

"What happened to Tori?" Jimmy asked.

"Got cleaned up, squeezed into this steampunk corset number," Vicki said, "Next thing she's done in, couldn't handle the swaying."

"We're tied to a dock," Jimmy said.

Vicki tossed up her hands. "Called a cab and that was it." Digging a folded paper from her stash pocket, she handed it to Jimmy. "Said call her if you want."

Frowning, Jimmy tucked it away, Vicki looking at Beck, saying, "He sign you up yet?"

"Been working on me."

"I'm in," she said, her eyes dancing, hands holding the T-shirt like maybe he hadn't seen it.

Beck turned to Jimmy. "Didn't mention that."

Jimmy just shrugged. "Not mine to tell."

"Ditched a couple of auditions, postponed my HEART commitments," she said, "but I'm all in."

"He mention how cold it gets, bottom of the world?"

"Got the parkas, right?" she asked.

"Yeah, Canada Goose all the way," Jimmy said. "Big logos on the pockets, look good for the cameras."

"Fresh-water rationing," Beck said, "He mention you'll be lining up for sponge baths, sharing a washcloth?"

"Nothing like that," Jimmy said, laughing.

"Three, four days in and you start smelling like a hamster."

"They're cute, right, hamsters?" she said, laughing too.

"All that to save a fish," Beck said.

"Mammals," they both said.

Beck felt the ship sway, the engines rumbling louder now, Beck knowing the sounds of a ship getting underway, looking at Jimmy, saying, "Full of surprises, huh?"

"My idea," she said, sitting next to Beck on the bunk, taking his hand, patting it, Jimmy draining his cup, setting it on the desk, asking Beck, "Sure I can't get you something else?"

"Maybe some ice . . . for my hand." Rubbing his knuckles.

"What's with your hand?" she asked, looking at it.

"Nothing yet," Beck said, looking at Jimmy.

Jimmy grinned at him, a jumbled announcement coming over the PA, something Beck couldn't make out.

Vicki kept patting Beck's hand, saying, "You took me on a boat ride, now it's my turn."

"This is you getting even, huh?"

"Just once around English Bay. Drinks up in a warm wheelhouse. Hardly makes us even."

"And dinner?" Beck said, looking at Jimmy.

"Right after some wine and vegan cheese. Get us started."

Jimmy was first through the doorway. Vicki hooked Beck's arm, leading the way, saying the milk-free cheddar was to die for.

... DEVIL'S IN THE BED

"So, I'm supposed to what, walk up, middle of the day, busy fucking marina," Eddie said. "Say 'how you doing, saw you naked,' and start shooting?"

The two of them at a table in the dining room, out of ear-shot from the two bikers shooting pool, Ramon picking up the sandwich Axel brought, Axel sticking his head through the kitchen door, asking if they wanted dills on the side. The old man had told Axel to keep an eye on them, even took Ramon's keys, his Town Car miles away at the truck rental place.

"Wouldn't mind," Ramon said, Axel ducking back into the kitchen. Making a pile of sandwiches after getting onto Transport Canada's website, looking up boat registrations, finding out about the boat, *Triggerfish*, showing the year the Grady-White was built, registered to one Rene Beckman. Had the home address as the Burrard Civic Marina, Axel saying, "Looks like your boy lives on board."

Taking a bite, Ramon lifted the top slice of bread, checked out the sandwich: bologna, mustard and mayo, slice of onion, iceberg or something like it. Not bad. A plate of potato salad next to it. Never had it with apple.

Eddie shook his head, asking, "That sound like me, Ramon?" First time he called him by name, not Uncle. Needing another line to ease out his nerves. "Just walk up and shoot a guy?"

Ramon shrugged like it didn't matter.

Eddie looked at the sandwich on his plate. Who could eat? The Taurus still over on the bar, Eddie hoping the piece of shit misfired. "Fucker says his sister would do this," Eddie kept his voice low, mimicked the way Diego said it, dragging his vowels, *sister* sounding like *seester*. "Then I say let her go to town."

"So why didn't you tell him?" Ramon said, chewing.

"What?"

"Get his sister to do it."

"That guy? You can't tell him shit. And what's with the one with the Elvis hair? Why's he got to come with?"

"Making sure it gets done."

Axel came back, set down a side of pickles, went back over to the bar. Doing some more searching online, finding out Beckman was an ex-cop, the guy stabbed in the line of duty, taking down some gun runners. Shit! Axel thinking he'd better go tell his old man. This shit getting deeper by the minute.

Ramon dropped the crust on his plate, took a pickle and crunched into it, glad he took his .357 from the boat, left it in the car under the seat. Just not sure how he would get to it, the car miles away at the truck rental joint.

Eddie thinking he could still run, sliding his plate over to Ramon.

"That one ham?"

"Yeah, with cheese."

Ramon taking it, biting into it, saving the potato salad for last.

"And why not you? You pissed him off. You do it."

"Didn't ask me," Ramon said, wiping his hands on the napkin. "Told me to drive. Best thing right now, kid, is chill."

"Chill?"

"As in shut the fuck up, let me think."

Eddie switched to sullen, thinking where he could run. Had his second cousin Juan in Calgary, a school buddy in Burlington, a chick he used to go with living out past Toronto, Bay of something; they kept up a Facebook thing. No way he was ending up like Uncle DeJesus, doing life behind bars, nothing to do but count the days. If he didn't run, maybe he could score some blow off Regular Joe, get so fucking wasted nobody in their right mind would send him after the naked guy.

Back behind the bar, Axel got on the phone, hoping for word on the three hundred guns, the two bikers shooting pool, drinking the old man's beer. The cartel crew showering and napping in their cabins out back. Rudi had gone out back to see Diego, trying to talk sense to him. Diego not understanding the problem: being an ex-cop was all the more reason to shoot the fucker in the head.

Ramon got up, clapped Eddie on the shoulder, telling him to relax, went to the fridge, seeing Axel on the phone. Helping himself to a couple of beers, he came back, set one in front of Eddie, told him to drink it. Sitting down, he grabbed another slice of dill, pulled the tab on his own beer.

. . . THIRD WHEEL

BECK FOLLOWED them down the passageway on the tween deck, taking the stairs on the starboard side, Jimmy leading the way to the bridge, on a roll, telling Vicki what life was like in the Southern Ocean.

"Dangling from that ladder, man, what a rush . . ." Jimmy said, "Really had to reach deep, know what I mean?"

Vicki said, "Oh, God," loving this, stepping next to him, her hand on Jimmy's arm.

Jimmy recounted how he crewed with the Sea Shepherds, able seaman on the *MY Steve Irwin* last season, telling how he climbed into the Zodiac, plunging through icy seas, taking it to the Japanese whalers. "One slip on an icy rung, and, man, I would've ended under nine hundred tons of whaler, chewed by giant props."

Beck thinking Jimmy was spinning a mix of Melville and Verne, throwing in a touch of *Pequod*. This asshole trying to make it with Vicki. Beck thinking he should have left her outside the Bay.

Taking the steps to the wheelhouse, Jimmy turned, was saying to her, "So we're in this inflatable, just a four-man crew, bobbing after them on waves high as hell. Minus-zero ice water splashing over the bow, biting through our Mustang suits."

"Oh, God."

"We see the masts of the *Nisshin Maru*," Jimmy said. "Rising like a tower three miles off, bearing down at seventeen knots. Our twin Mercs screaming, our Zodiac popping from the water, us giving chase."

Vicki touched her chest, turned to Beck.

Jimmy kept talking, "Plunging and hopping like a PNE ride. On my feet, yelling, a bottle of acid in my hand. Closing the gap, dodging the growlers."

Vicki wanting to know what that was.

"Killer ice, size of a city bus."

"Oh, my God."

"Hit one and you're done."

"Where's this vegan place?" Beck asked her.

"*Shh.*" Then back to Jimmy.

Jimmy saying that's when he spotted the harpoon ship bearing down on them. "Half mile off our stern, their LRAD screaming."

"Let me get this," Beck said, bottom of the steps, "Hundred tons of steel, harpoons and spray cannons against you and your rubber boat and bottle of rotten butter."

"Butyric acid," Jimmy said.

"These guys running from you?"

"Believe me, you don't want that shit all over your deck . . ."

"Stop it, Beck," Vicki said. "Go on, Jimmy."

Jimmy reached for the door, music coming from inside

the wheelhouse, something by Three Dog Night. "Got right under the giant bow, water cannons jetting all over us."

Not following up the steps, Beck turned to the rail, looking to the North Shore Mountains, betting Jimmy got all this from watching *Animal Planet*. Tori was the smart one, leaving when she did, Beck remembering he was supposed to call Hattie, fillet of spring salmon in his fridge.

Shit.

"We're throwing acid; me, I'm dangling the prop-fouling line, tossing it out, feeling it take, wrapping around their monster prop . . ." Jimmy holding the door open, Vicki following him, Jimmy talking, the music pumping.

This ain't the way to have fun.

•

DAMP SEA air and fog settled in. Didn't matter the drizzle started. A four-man inflatable and a pair of Jet Skis were lashed to the foredeck. Forearms on the starboard rail, Beck made out the line of lights going up Lonsdale. A SeaBus angled across the harbor, ferrying the nine-to-fivers home. Stanley Park at his back going from green to purple, the anti-whaler passing under the girders of the Lions Gate, cars up top rushing between downtown and the North Shore.

Couldn't figure Vicki out, inviting him to dinner, near-naked on a downtown street, not saying Jimmy was coming along. Signing up to save whales.

Testing the engines, the engineer was doing a loop in the Strait of Georgia, Captain Angus getting looped on wine and alternative cheese, a microphone in hand, Beck hearing him drumming up support from the who's who up in the wheelhouse. The breeze was picking up, squawking gulls circling, sounded like they were laughing at him, the foam washing off the bow.

The drizzle brought a chill, Beck going from thoughts of Vicki Moon to Ashika Shakira, thinking back to the night the woman stabbed him — something that woke him and left him in a cold sweat many a night. Beck remembering those eyes, the feeling of the blade going in. Wondering if he could have pulled the trigger. Put a bullet in a woman. Beck guessing she fled across the border the same night she left him in critical condition, the woman long gone by the time the medics stopped the bleeding. Good chance they'd never catch her.

Beck noticed the two skinny guys in crew T-shirts on the upper deck call to him, the pair leaning on mops, guessing him for a fresh recruit set to heave his guts over the side, a couple hundred yards from shore.

The taller one was saying, "Wait till you get a load of the Roaring Forties, mate."

Both of them killing themselves laughing, doubling over their mops.

Beck threw them a look, then a finger, not sure what a Roaring Forty was. He fished in a pocket for his cell, pressed the speed dial for Hattie. Seeing Vicki step from the wheelhouse, coming down the steps, he clicked off the phone, wiping the wet from his forehead.

Stepping to the rail next to him, a plastic wineglass in hand, rolled T-shirt pinned under her arm, she glanced at the two guys above, saying, "Making friends, huh?" She waved to them, calling, "Hey, Nemo. Hey, Knut."

The two hands tripped into each other, as nerdy as their names, both waving back.

"Didn't tell me we were pulling anchor," he said, dropping his cell in the pocket.

"Took me on a boat ride; now I'm taking you on one. Only we'll make it back without needing a tow." Hooking her arm through his, she gestured toward the shore, the lights of Ambleside twinkling in the mist, a lone figure tossing a crab pot off the end of a pier. "Pretty, huh?"

"Yeah."

Bumping him with a hip, she said, "Don't do the wet blanket, okay?" Offered him her wineglass.

Sipping from it, he looked at her. "What's the thing with Jimmy?"

"Just friends." Taking the glass back, she started up the steps, saying, "Captain's got canapés."

Beck caught her arm, pulling her to him, wine spilling.

She pressed the rolled T against him, saying, "Think I got your size right."

He held it up, *ANTARCTICA CREW* across the back. "Funny."

"Could be, with you on board." She set the glass on the deck, slipped her hands under his shirt, lifting it. Drizzle coming down.

Stopping her hands, Beck aimed his thumb at the two deckhands on the top deck. Like maybe she forgot they were there.

"Nothing they haven't seen before," she said, smoothing his shirt down.

He caught her hands, drew her close, Vicki letting it happen, kissing him, the lights from shore playing on the water, waves swishing against the bull-nose hull, drizzle coming down.

"Come with," she said, last night's anger gone, grinning, playing with him.

"Got my own boat, business to run."

"Think catching salmon beats saving whales?"

"Think your fish are big enough to take care of themselves."

"Mammals, not fish." Vicki flicked a finger at his lip, saying, "Jimmy saw a cow and her calf harpooned right in front of their boat last year."

"Ship, not boat," Beck said.

Pulling away, she took her wine and went up the metal steps, this girl wearing heels on a ship. She pulled the wheelhouse door, the sound of the Doobies pouring out, talking 'bout China Grove. She looked back at him, saying, "You know it's raining, right, Beck?"

Then she was gone.

Taking out his ringing cell, Beck looked at the display, no idea what to say to Hattie, dropping it back in his pocket.

The ship's engines slowed, Beck felt the ship coming about.

. . . HEAVY COVER

THE SUB was moored along the rotting pier, the hull covered
with soggy chunks of old planks, kelp fronds, boughs of cedar
and bramble, piled to hide the conning tower. Done under
the cover of night, the spot Ramon found.

A dozen bales of *cocaína* down in the steel hull, Ismael
Rios Chavez sat up top, feet dangling down the hatch,
keeping watch. First sight of a police boat and his orders
were to scuttle the sub. Diego's orders. Fucker too dumb to
realize the sub was sitting too shallow, its bottom on the silt.

The only chance if he were spotted was to make a run.
But for that he needed an extra pair of hands, Ismael wanting
to keep Reyes aboard. Diego saying no, fearing the two
Hondurans would take off. So here he was, a sitting duck.

All that *cocaína* and a crate of grenades at the bottom
of the ladder. Dead Carlos down there getting ripe. No
middle names, no last name, no idea about Carlos, just a
Colombian fisherman looking for something better. Guy
never said two words. Died after they entered Canadian
waters, while Ismael manned the controls. Ismael guessing
the Colombian couldn't take the heat, had to be a hundred

degrees the whole time they were underway, the crew sucking foul air for eleven days, thick and wet, not much oxygen. They would dump his body once they were back out at sea, hooking up with the cargo ship *Costas,* which would refuel them and replace their batteries.

Then he was thinking of the bikers that thought themselves hard men. Bikers like in *Easy Rider.* Ismael would like to show them what growing up on the streets of a Honduran coastal town was about, Ismael learning to dive for the lobster when he was six, watching school friends drown, stealing from market carts to stay alive. Killed his first man when he was thirteen, a jefe refusing to pay him his half day of wages. Snatching the *facón* from the fat man's own belt, Ismael pushed it in, nothing to it, looking at the man, the jefe grunting, his knees buckling, with the light going from his eyes. Went through his pockets and took what he was owed and a little extra. And ran.

The laughing *puto* was next, in the San Pedro Sula prison. Ismael did it with just a piece of rusted steel. Pulled it from the back of his bunk, honed it on the stone floor, fashioned a handle from a patch of shirt, stuck the sharpened end in the man's liver in the prison yard and walked away, the guards watching from their side of the yellow line, the line of death. Killed three more, not an inmate or jailer laughing at Ismael for the rest of his stay in the San Pedro Sula, the Valley of the Birds, where the inmates ran the prison.

Recruited upon his release, he was trained in Texas by his new CIA friends who taught him to kill with more than rusted steel. They had him placed at the marine infantry base in Coveqas, training with the Colombians, learning about submarines.

After the *americanos* punched his ticket back to San Pedro Sula, he was appointed to the Death Squad, applying what he'd been taught, working the secret jails of his country. Nearly a hundred citizens stood before him, mostly leftist dissidents, made to stand naked in damp cells, rats and roaches for company. Ismael had them chained to walls, whipped and beaten, filthy water thrown when they blacked out, spoiled food tossed on the floor.

For two years Ismael kept the rebel tongues wagging, the English priest taking the longest, Ismael using electrical shock. The smell of the man's pale flesh burning filled the cell, his screams becoming moans near the end.

Receiving penance at the Church of Christ, Ismael kneeled at the confessional, saying the Hail Marys, forgiven by another priest, of his own faith. It was his last day with the Death Squad.

Two men approached him at a cafe a week later, asked to sit at his table and told him about a submarine being built in the jungles of Ecuador, said they were looking for good men, talked about more money than he ever dreamed. Pushed an envelope stuffed with cash toward him.

Ismael looked at it, then at the men.

A dozen runs behind him now, working for the cartel bosses, all had gone without a hitch. Ismael thinking he should have been put in charge of this one, the Baja Maritanos wanting one of their own, Lieutenant Topo giving the nod to Diego, the Mexican knowing shit about submarines.

And now here he was, Ismael sitting on the sidelines, taking orders from Diego, the crisscrossed cedar boughs hiding him from view, affording him a three-hundred-and-sixty-degree vantage.

...A HIT'S A HIT

LATE AFTERNOON sun edged from behind the dark clouds. Amado climbed across the seat, getting out of the rental truck, arching his back, stretching.

They went into the Fifth Wheel, taking a booth by the window, Ramon and Eddie sitting across from him, Amado telling the waitress he wanted coffee, the girl going for the pot, Amado checking her out. Coming back, she set down mugs, pouring coffee like she'd done it a million times, pointed to the creamers and sugar packets in the trolley, asked if they wanted anything else and hurried off.

"Okay, here's how I see this," Eddie said. "We go down, give this guy the thumping of his life, all three of us. Wave the pistol in his face, let him know we're not fucking around."

Tasting his coffee, Amado tore a sugar packet and threw it in, swished his mug around, adding another sugar, finally saying, "In head," tapping his temple. Guessing Eddie would piss his pants finding out the target was ex-police. Diego's order was not to tell them till after.

Putting cream in his, Eddie watched it swirl, took a sip, looking at his uncle, then out the window. Wishing he could stoke a pissed-off feeling. This asshole coming up here in a sub built in the Amazon, shitting in a bucket, telling them how things were.

Ramon said nothing, told to sit in the passenger seat, Eddie to drive them to the marina. Returning the rental truck on the way, swapping it for the Town Car — his .357 under the seat — Ramon taking it one step at a time.

"So, Amado," Ramon said finally, "what corner of old Mexico you from?"

That got him a look.

"Been to Puerto Vallarta a couple times." Ramon mispronouncing it, saying, "Folks hustling time-shares, wearing those big fucking hats, everybody with a hand out for a tip, stray dogs with ribs showing, half of them hit by cars with no exhaust. People not giving a shit. You from a place like that?"

Amado pulled a smoke from a pack of Faros *con filtro* and lit up, waved out the match, looking at him. He blew smoke across the table, a vein making the prison-tat on his neck jump.

"Thinking of going back down," Ramon said. "Maybe Cabo this time."

Amado looking at him.

Ought to hang warning signs on these guys. Eddie tossed a couple bucks on the table and got up, a pair of truckers in baseball caps glancing over on account of Amado's cigarette smoke, complaining about it, the waitress on her way, the manager behind her, neither of them bringing an ashtray. Eddie going out the door, still thinking he should run.

DROPPING THE truck at the Budget lot, the three of them walked to Ramon's Lincoln, a Town Car from the eighties, faded burgundy with a brown vinyl roof. Amado stopped Ramon from getting behind the wheel, pointing at Eddie, going to the passenger side, climbing in back, asking what car this was, trying to crack open the fake vent window.

"Vintage Town Car, amigo," Ramon said, his .357 within reach. Getting in, he turned in the passenger seat, serious about his ride, telling Amado this one had the Rolls-Royce grille, built like a brick shithouse, Amado agreeing it was shit, couldn't find a crank or button that opened the rear window, sticking a cigarette in his mouth.

"Can't smoke in here," Ramon said, the Mexican lighting up behind him. For all his chain-smoking, Ramon never lit up in the Town Car, never once. Rubbing and polishing with Armor All and Turtle Wax. Taking a cheesecloth to her. Smoke rolled along the headliner, Ramon cracking his window, the rosary dangling from the rearview.

Eddie gave a sideways glance at Ramon, his uncle just letting it happen. Bucket shitter in back of his ride, smoking, telling them who to kill.

Eddie held the crate at fifty-five, feeling a shimmy through the steering column, the back-belch of exhaust notes mixing with Mexican tobacco. Traffic built toward the north end of Surrey, the *Welcome to Vancouver* sign tagged, *Stolen Land* sprayed across it. Amado lay across the rear seat, smoking, then snoring as they rolled along the Number One.

Eddie looked at Ramon, thinking no way Uncle DeJesus would let this greaser pull any of this shit. Thinking Ramon was getting soft.

"Take Grandview," Ramon told him, Eddie driving past it, flicking a finger at the dangling rosary. He took First, getting caught at every light, the rush hour traffic heavy. Turning on Clark, he headed down to Broadway, made another wrong turn on a one-way, ending bumper to bumper with an Econoline, the guy behind the wheel honking, throwing his arms, pointing at the one-way sign, Ramon telling Eddie to chill, just to back her up.

Pulling into the parking lot at the back end of Granville Island, Eddie was feeling sick, telling Ramon they parked in the wrong spot, should be over by Burrard, Ramon telling him to shut up. Fishing change from a pocket, he got out and fed the meter.

Climbing from the back, Amado muttered, "*Pedazo de mierda.*" Left his butts stamped out on the floor mat. Stepping between the Lincoln and a Pontiac wagon, he unzipped and let loose a stream of piss, sighing his relief, splashing Ramon's front right wheel.

Eddie couldn't believe these guys, marking their territory. Ramon let that slide, too, leading the way, the three of them walking like tourists, passing Arts Umbrella, a sign pointing to Emily Carr. A catering place called The Butler Did It was getting a delivery, a guy with a backwards Canucks cap wheeling a stack of boxes on a cart.

A slip of a park with kids playing on a swing set. Shopkeepers kneeling in a window, working on a display, placing jugs and vases. Deep reds and earthy browns popular this season. A souvenir place boasted everything Vancouver, a for-sale sign in the next window. A tour group climbed off a sightseeing bus, going through the double doors of the brewery, shoppers strolling to the Market. Eddie saying again they parked in the wrong spot.

"Island's a magnet for tourists," Ramon said to Amado. "No stray dogs here, amigo."

"Why is called an island?" Amado said, the place attached to the mainland.

Ramon grinned at him, then said to Eddie, "You know, kid, you're right. This's the wrong spot." Turning back, telling them to go on, walk past the marina, said he was getting the car, meet them past the Burrard Bridge, park by the marina. Gone before Amado could object.

Alone with the Mexican, Eddie felt the panic rise. Walking by the Clam Up, a cafe and oyster bar, the waft of garlic shrimp coming from the place, Eddie thinking everybody passing could see the piece under Amado's shirt. Could be Ramon was taking off, leaving him.

Past the Granville Bridge, they took the walkway, sailboat masts sticking up like barren trees. Low tide, seagulls and crows hunting between wet rocks, the evening coming on, a breeze blowing off the Pacific. Joggers in Lululemon outfits, mothers with jogging strollers, couples walking arm in arm.

Didn't say a word until they were past the Burrard Bridge. Taking a flight of wooden steps by the marina, Eddie felt relief, catching sight of the Lincoln pulling onto Whyte, Ramon with his shades on, coaxing the old wreck into a parking spot, nobody seeing him reach under the seat, tucking the AMT Backup in his windbreaker.

Looking at Ramon's ride, Amado said, "Is a true piece of shit."

Hard to argue that, Eddie thought.

Ramon getting out. The three of them taking the steps and walking along the pier, checking the names on the transoms. Stopping at the Grady-White, *Triggerfish* written across the stern, cartoon of a fish, *Coho-a-go-go.com* under it.

Hosing the aft deck, Griff looked at the three men, navy cap on his head, *Triggerfish* across the brim, same cartoon fish, Beck's tinted shades over his eyes, getting her ready for an early-morning charter. Making sure the batteries were charged.

"Evening, gents," Griff said, taking them for tourists.

Ramon nodded, peeling off his glasses, hooking them on his shirt, Amado looking around, as friendly as a plague, Eddie with the nervous eyes, his hands in his windbreaker pockets. Leaning close, he said to Ramon, "This ain't the guy."

Same hat with the fish, same yellow shades. Ramon told Eddie, "*Shhh.*"

"How can I help?" Griff tried again, stopped what he was doing, turning off the water.

"Like to take in English Bay, see some sights," Ramon said, putting on a smile.

"Yeah, when are you thinking?" Griff said.

"We're here, right?" Ramon said, smiling.

"Sorry, we're closed," Griff told him. "Business hours are ten till —"

Amado stepped onboard, bumping past him, sitting by the helm, fishing out a cigarette, lighting up and spreading his arms across the back of the surround seating. Ramon followed suit, sitting opposite. Eddie got on last.

"Won't keep you out late, promise," Ramon said, fishing a native smoke from his pack, flicking his lighter, lighting his, then Amado's.

"See, I so much as bend the rules . . ." Griff started to say.

"Bending beats breaking, am I right?" Ramon reached in a pocket, taking out his roll, peeling off a few bills, holding them out to Griff. "Ought to cover any bent rules."

Eddie leaned close, saying again this wasn't their guy, Ramon telling him to sit quiet.

"Just a quick tour, right?" Pocketing the bills, rolling the hose, Griff tossed it on the dock, feeling these guys were all wrong.

"All we ask," Ramon said, smiling at him.

"Should mention, skipper was a cop," Griff said, knowing he didn't have a choice.

"That so?" Ramon said, guessing it was bullshit.

"Everything okay, Griff?" Hattie called over from the *First Light*, a mug in her hand, looking from under her Tilley hat.

"Yeah, yeah, all good, Hattie." Griff waved and went about casting off the lines, not wanting her involved, Ramon and Amado looking over at her, both thinking, could be the girl they saw naked Friday evening. Amado thinking he'd take care of her as soon as they got back. Should be near dark by then.

Sitting in her deck chair, Hattie watched Beck's mate out-stepping his bounds, taking *Triggerfish* out, three passengers on board, none of them looking right. Griff took her out solo day before yesterday, Beck running around for the girl that wore heels on a boat. Likely chasing her now, blowing off their dinner plans, letting Griff take care of business. She watched him cast off, standing at the console, flipping the light switches. Hattie with a bad feeling.

. . . ON A DEAD SEA

CLOUDS HUNG heavy, bringing on the early dusk. Chop that started out light, waves capping now just past Vanier Park. Working his trembling hand, Griff tapped enough throttle to plane her out, heading into English Bay. Not sure what these guys wanted. Had to do with Beck: maybe payback from his cop days. Lunatics he put behind bars.

Freaking, heart pounding, he kept his eyes forward, hand on the throttle, trying to be cool. The radio's handset within reach. Beck's nine-millimeter Sig in the forward hatch down in the V-berth. Not sure what to do, telling himself it was better to shoot than be shot. The dark-skinned guy with the pomp kept his eyes on him, felt like they were burning through Griff, like he knew what he was thinking.

The older one was asking if that was the girl on the other boat, Griff saying what girl? Passing Spanish Banks to the south, Spirit Park coming up, Griff kept his heading for the Strait, shoving away the fear, planning his move. Talking over the engine's rumble, he said to Ramon, "See there, rain coming. Likely get rough. You fellows want, I can circle by

Lighthouse Park, take in the inner harbor. Be calmer in there. Get to see some city lights."

Amado pointed straight out to sea, nodded to Eddie, telling him in Spanish to get it done. Pointing at his temple. Getting up, he passed Eddie the piece so Griff couldn't see and stepped to the rail, set his feet apart, and pulled his zipper down. Amado pissing all the time.

"Too close to shore," Eddie said, looking at the university lands to the south.

Ramon said nothing, Eddie tucking the Taurus under his leg, hiding it from Griff.

Pissing again, a symptom of the prostate troubles the Mexican doctor warned him about, Amado splashed the deck where Griff just swabbed, nodded for Eddie to get it done.

Eddie got up. Griff's eyes went wide seeing the pistol. He fought the fear, saying, "Look man, I'm telling you, a cop owns this boat." The locator beacon was in the compartment with the fire extinguisher. Maybe he could switch it on, bounce a distress signal. Maybe he could get to Beck's gun . . .

Zipping up, Amado snapped his fingers, meaning for Eddie to hurry up. Then he went rummaging through the deck compartments, pulling stuff out: a flashlight, a searchlight, fleece, flask, totes, a couple of life jackets, length of nylon rope, a dry bag. Something to weigh the body down when they pitched it overboard. Tossing it all out on the deck.

"You just say what you're after, maybe I can help," Griff said, eyes never leaving the pistol barrel. The guy holding it looked scared, too, Griff not sure he had it in him. It was the guy with the greasy pomp running the show, going through the compartments, crabbing around on his knees.

Griff gave up on minding the helm, *Triggerfish* off course, bobbing in a trough, the sea getting higher. Pushing up from the aft seat, Ramon stepped past Griff and took the wheel, turning her into the wind, giving it some throttle.

The last compartment housed the row of batteries. Amado ripped out a set of cables, clunking a battery on the deck. Getting up, sucking at a cut on his hand, he told Eddie one more time to get it done.

Staring into the barrel took the last of his resolve. A dark stain spread across Griff's crotch.

"Telling you he's the wrong guy," Eddie said again, his palm wet on the Taurus's grip.

Amado came at him, landing a slap, cursing him.

Eddie staggered, turned the pistol on him. "Don't want to do that, you greasy . . ."

Amado grinned, snatching the pistol from him, only now noticing Ramon at the helm with the small pistol in his hand, pointing it at Amado, smiling at him, saying, "One thing we got to clear up, amigo."

Amado lost the grin, standing there, aiming at the wrong guy.

"The Lincoln Town Car's one classic ride, with or without the Rolls-Royce grille. I want to hear you say it."

"Is a piece of shit," Amado said, betting he could wheel and fire before Ramon got off a shot.

"Gonna say you're sorry for stinking her up."

Amado spun to fire.

The shot backed him up, Amado looking down, blood spreading across his shirt. His breath caught, and he tried to raise the Taurus.

"Gonna take me a month to get that stench off my uphol-stery," Ramon said, firing again, putting Amado on his back, the Taurus dropping to the deck, Griff edging toward the rail.

Amado felt the drizzle on his face — cold, not like the rain that came off the Gulf back home.

Ramon watched Amado Garza die, mouth open, cater-pillar eyebrows over the Manson eyes staring up at the rain. Then he looked to where Eddie pointed; Griff had gone over the side. Tossing the Taurus as far as he could into the angry sea, Ramon dropped the AMT back in his pocket and took the wheel, getting *Triggerfish* straightened out in the four-foot swells. The only ship he could see was too far to the east for anyone to have heard the shots, *RESEARCH* painted down its starboard side, the ship heading for the Lions Gate.

Making a few passes, they searched for Griff. Giving up, Ramon switched on the Lowrance and headed the Grady-White for the deeper troughs, telling Eddie to tie the Mexican to the battery and make it tight.

Eddie did it, moving mechanically, slipping the rope under the dead man, binding Amado to the battery.

Hoisting the body, they dropped him over the side, watching him disappear, the Mexican's eyes open, staring back at them, fading in the murk.

Taking the wheel, Ramon told Eddie to clean the mess on the deck. Riding the swells, he headed to port, couldn't make out the lighthouse at Point Atkinson through the sheet of rain coming down now. Crossing the Strait, he started thinking how he'd sell the story to Rudi and the one called Diego.

. . . LUCKING OUT

THE PLACE was called Jaggery's, a nice atmosphere with a juice bar, good selection of salads under a bank of lights, everything fresh, black-and-white Kubrick prints on a brick wall. A chalkboard showed the daily vegan specials, the place going for a hip minimalist look, sax jazz not too loud through mounted speakers, Paul Desmond or somebody like that. The waitress looked like she scraped by on tofu and rice, skinny and pale, blonde dreads tied back, had that student-working-her-way-through-school look.

Vicki sat between Beck and Jimmy in the corner booth, calling them her boys. Raising a toast, she clinked glasses and sipped her carrot-orange smoothie, licking the froth from her lip, being cute about it, bopping to the jazz. Saying she would miss the "You say Meat, I say Murder" campaign, on account of saving whales with Jimmy and the Sea Rangers. Saying what a blast it was working with HEART, recounting the time they wrapped her up like a tray of meat, Saran Wrap with slits so she could breathe, left her on the sidewalk out front of the art gallery.

"Wearing nothing but Saran Wrap?" Beck said.

"As a matter of fact . . ."

Beck checked the clock by the juice bar, the lettering around the face told him it was time for wild krill oil, Beck not sure why he was hanging around this vegan place without a liquor license, feeling like the odd man out, thinking he should have called Hattie a couple hours back, made up some excuse.

Tasting his green shake, Jimmy said, "Take it Officer Beck disapproves of HEART?"

"Like most of us with a Y chromosome," Beck said, "I'd pay to see her naked." Sipping his apple pie smoothie.

"How much?" she said.

"I don't know, what's the going rate?"

Downing the last of his green drink, Jimmy held the glass up to the waitress, saying to hit him again, then to Vicki, "So, what's the craziest thing you get asked?"

"With HEART?" She thought, saying, "Know what I get a lot? People asking when's Pam coming out."

"Anderson? Come on, she's had her day, got nothing on you."

"You kidding? Everybody wants Pam."

"Seriously, she'd pale."

"You're sweet." Squeezing Jimmy's cheek, she said, "Did a gig with her one time."

"Yeah?"

"Save-a-Seal rally. Stood right next to her when she posted the petition on behalf of HEART. That girl drummed up like half-a-million signatures. Hundreds turned up at the art gallery just to watch her lick the stamp, sending it on its way to Ottawa. Something like a dozen news cameras going off as she dropped it in the box, showing the cleavage and giving that big smile. Posing the whole while with her back nice and straight. Can't even tell you how many tweets that got."

"Sorry I missed it. What say, Beck?"

"I say we order." Studying the sandwich board, Beck asked what kind of dip came with the crudités.

Vicki saying, "The dips are dairy-free, and, I swear, you say one more thing, think I'll —"

"What, get naked?"

Play-slapping his arm, saying he was being just awful.

Beck asked what tian was.

"It's good, you should go for it," she said. "Goes nice with the vichyssoise."

More diners stepped in, remnants of the after-work crowd, two guys in jackets and ties, their dates dolled up. The waitress got them seated by the window, coming over with her pad and pencil, giving a smile.

"Vichyssoise, that's what, cold potato, right?" Beck asked, the waitress saying yeah, but the cook did it with leek and watercress in a veggie broth. Beck thinking, throw in some bacon, serve it with scotch, and he'd be all set.

"Put me down for the Sloppy Jane," Jimmy said, not needing the board.

The girl, writing on her pad, asked TVP, tofu or tempeh, Jimmy going with the tempeh, asking for baby arugula on the side.

Vicki going for the sun-dried heirlooms on a porto,

topped with basil pesto, a side of sprouted almonds and cracked filberts. The waitress put Beck down for a Sloppy Jane, too, then headed for the pass window.

Jimmy saying how the Sea Rangers kicked off every day with a Dr. Oz, the galley crew dishing up one mean tofu scramble, fixing it any way you liked.

Twisting the cap off his mineral water, Beck thought he might give Danny Green a call, get him to run a check, see if Jimmy really did two tours, saying he read the Japanese weren't even whaling this year.

"They always say that," Jimmy said, going on about water cannons and concussion grenades till the waitress brought their food, setting the plates down, Jimmy forking Sloppy Jane into his mouth, talking around it, telling how they kept the Japanese from harvesting a single whale for eighteen days straight last season, staying on the factory ship's ass, knocking their quota off by a mile.

Beck asked Jimmy to pass the salt, telling Vicki the vegan food wasn't bad. The waitress came asking about dessert, saying the no-bake chocolate torte was to die for, Beck asking if it had real chocolate, the girl giving him a look, saying she'd be back.

Vicki started talking about Dimples and the how how how and boom boom boom, same story Beck already heard, Jimmy laughing about it. Beck's cell gave that old-school ring. Leaning and taking it from his pocket, he looked at the display. It was Hattie. Beck guessing this was about getting stood up for dinner, that nice fillet of spring salmon.

"Man. You won't believe what happened —" Beck started to say.

"You need get over here." Worry in her voice.

Almost slipped, saying he was just about to order dessert — sitting here with the girl with the heels, saying, "What's up?"

"Jesus, Beck, get here, as in right now!"

. . . AIRTIGHT

Lights of the city glowed above the dark of Stanley Park, False Creek coming up, the night air getting colder by the minute, *Triggerfish*'s engines rumbling.

Calm for a guy that just shot somebody, first time in his life, Ramon thinking Amado made it easy. Bringing the boat in, doing double the five knots allowed, saying to Eddie, "Where the fuck we going to run?"

"Figure it out as we go." His hands stuck under his armpits, Eddie couldn't help shaking. The bridge was up ahead, the Burrard Civic Marina beyond it. "Main thing, we get the hell away."

"With no money?" Ramon shook his head.

"These fuckers are crazy. Not going to say shit happens and forget about it."

Ramon concocting a plan. "We say Beckman pulled a piece; you shot him, and I jumped in, tried to stop it, his gun went off and Amado caught the bullet. Nothing to be done for it."

"Wasn't even Beckman."

"And the Mexican won't be here long enough to find that out."

"Still say we run. Get in your car and go."

"Ever live on the run?" Ramon said. "Me with my oil pump shot, Firestones bald as melons. Nothing in the account. How far you think we'd get?"

"Least it's living."

"We spin this right, we're golden. And Rudi needs us working the tug, plus me and him go back."

"Rudi's a psycho, same as the Mexican. And you shot their guy — twice."

"Three times. But we tell it like I said, Beckman shot Amado, poor guy getting pitched over the side. Maybe hit his head, I don't know. We searched, but with the chop and it getting dark, he didn't come up."

"Suppose Beckman's guy does?"

"Far out as he was, waves this high, undertows and currents. Mark Spitz couldn't make it from that far out."

No idea Mark Spitz was part fish, eleven Olympic medals to prove it, Eddie looked doubtful.

"Plus Rudi's going to put it on Diego, guy insisting this Beckman takes a bullet. Ask me, the Mexican gets his guns, he's out of here. Case closed."

"And the woman watching back at the dock. Four guys go out, two come back."

"Why we're tying her up behind the Market and just walking away." Reaching for his native smokes, Ramon fished for a match, not finding one, asking Eddie for a light, Eddie patting his pockets, shaking his head.

Ramon needed to think, come at it from all angles. Rudi wouldn't like it, killing the guy and leaving the woman alive, but he had bigger things to worry about: all that coke in the bunker, more on the sub, three hundred Chinese AKs somewhere on a container ship, the cartel waiting. It was Diego, the guy with a burr up his ass after Ramon slapped his gun hand down back in the bay Friday night, kept him from shooting the naked couple right then.

The marina lay quiet. Passing under the Granville Bridge, Ramon pulled *Triggerfish* along the dock back of the Market, Eddie jumping on the dock and tying her off behind an Aquabus.

Lights along False Creek danced in the water, the last of the shoppers long gone. Every place on the island locked up, signs over doorways dark, the parking spaces empty.

Shoes scraped on the pavement, a handwritten sign by Market Seafood said they had wild sockeye, just in. A fat security guard strolled their way, whistling, making his rounds, saying it was a nice evening, his walkie-talkie squawking, the guy talking into it, didn't give them a second look.

Passing under the Granville girders, same way Eddie and Amado had walked earlier, they took the walkway past the sailing masts, path lights marking the way, the tide high now, a teenaged couple making out on a park bench.

They got to the Town Car. Getting in, Ramon stuck the cigarette in his mouth, fished a fresh pack of smokes from the glovebox, wedged the pistol back under the seat. Never let a soul smoke in his ride, the dead Mexican stinking it up, not respecting a man's personal property. Ramon feeling righteous that he shot him, thumbing in the lighter, never used it before, the ashtray stuffed with Doublemint wrappers and toothpicks.

Ramon turned the car onto Chestnut, blowing smoke out his window, tapping the cigarette in the ashtray, a gum wrapper catching fire, saying, "It's the right move, kid."

. . . LINE IN THE SAND

THE WHISKEY was local-made and cheap, stuff he funneled into cc bottles, left over from the days when hunters were too drunk to notice. Rudi looked at Diego, poured him a shot. "You going to tell me or not?" Rudi counted to five, getting his temper in check. Bad enough, this smelly bastard was drinking his cut-rate booze, playing the man in charge, sending Ramon and Eddie with the other greaser to shoot some boater turned out to be an ex-cop, putting the whole operation at risk.

Billy Wall looked over, Regular Joe clacking balls, shooting eight-ball on the table that set Rudi back five Gs, nice green felt with a slate bed, the Clydesdale fixture hanging over it.

The Honduran called Reyes leaned by the rack, a long-neck in his hand, checking out Rudi's trophy moose.

Lifting his leg, Regular Joe leaned across the table, his porkpie tilted, taking his shot, waiting for a ball to drop, cursing and slamming his fist on the felt.

Finished the five-count, Rudi looked at Diego, saying, "Need you to say more, brother." The Mexican got new instructions on his last call to his Lieutenant Topo, Diego telling Rudi they had a passenger to put on the sub. All he would say was it was a woman.

"*Salud.*" Tipping the drink back, Diego set it down, saying, "You get my guns, and you bring the woman if I say you bring the woman." Not telling him about Ashika Shakira, calling herself Camilla now, topping the RCMP's most-wanted list, the cartel wanting her to run the guns, Rudi and the bikers looking like amateurs. Diego's way of letting this gringo know who he was. Didn't put up with shit from Ismael either, Diego leaving him back on the sub. Diego answering to Topo Quintero, the man calling himself *el teniente*, the one who told him to bring the woman.

"Not sure you're reading me, amigo . . ." Rudi set the bottle down, counted five again, resting his forearms on the bar, thinking he could snap this man's spine, saying, "You think I'm hiding some woman on your say-so, and you not saying who she is . . ." He shook his head.

"How it is," Diego said it matter of fact, showing his hands.

Leaning close, not counting to five, Rudi put a hand under the bar, touching the length of pipe he used to straighten out drunken hunters back in the day. He considered how Travis Rainey would play this: his old pal who put the Sabers together with the Baja Maritanos in the first place. Started running cartel blow up from the Gulf, trucking it across two borders. Tons of the shit packed in Kinder Surprise making its way across the western States. Taught the border guards to wave and look the other way.

Truckloads of it ended up at Rudi's Hunt Lodge back

before the Sabers MC went down to Crown prosecutors, half its members doing time, the rest patching over to the Rockers, Rudi and Travis going partners on a property up in Pemberton, a distress sale on the Inn Between. Rudi and Travis figuring out folks in the northland loved to play pass the mirror same as anybody else. Rudi and Travis doing alright, trafficking in the north country, the inn fronting as a nice getaway for tourists.

If Travis Rainey had a hand in it, things turned golden. Never busted, never robbed. Everybody making money. Cartel and bikers happy. All except the last time.

The way Rudi heard it, Travis was lying low after signing up with Bumpy Rosco's outfit, knocking heads with the Indo Army out of Surrey, both laying claim to Whistler's drug trade after the Sabers went down. They painted the resort town bloody, and Rosco's son was gunned down, Travis Rainey taking the heat, old man Rosco laying blame and putting out a contract.

Knowing how Rosco would play it, Travis slipped into the shadows and disappeared. Travis not so golden that time; still, Rudi sure could use him here now, considering how Travis would handle this Mexican sitting in front of him.

Rudi's eldest son, Max, was already up in Pemberton with a hundred pounds packed behind the panels of his Econoline. Regular Joe and Billy Wall were set to take a truckload out of there at first light, but Diego held back six hundred pounds on the sub, on account of the delayed guns, the bikers not wanting to make the run six hundred pounds light.

Word was the cargo ship from North Korea was now in the harbor, waiting to dock. And the new plan was give it one more day. Now this Mexican was playing games, having boaters shot, wanting to hide some woman at his lodge, put her on board the sub, not saying who she was or why she needed hiding.

Regular Joe was looking over, saying something to Billy Wall, Billy looking over, too. Last thing Rudi needed was for shit to start in here. Fifteen hundred pounds of blow under the ground out back and these guys set to butt heads. Staring at Diego, Rudi tried again, saying, "This shit goes bad, it's on you."

Sliding the metal case close, never taking his eyes from Rudi, Diego flipped it open again and took out the sat phone, sticking in the battery and making another call, spoke in Spanish, said *sí* a couple of times, then hung up, finally saying to Rudi, "She is Hezbollah."

Rudi thought a moment, saying, "Wanted?"

"To us, she is wanted to help with the guns," Diego said, the Rockers not getting it done.

"And you want to put her on the sub?"

Diego nodded, removed the battery, put the phone back in the case.

"Always good knowing how deep the shit you're standing in's." Rudi refilled Diego's glass. "And this Hezbollah chick's got a price on her head?"

Diego nodded again. "You bring her here and another five thousand comes to you." He knocked back the shot, slid the glass forward. The five thousand was his own idea — improvising. Glad he left Ismael on the sub. The Honduran had a way of winding him up, second-guessing everything.

Rudi refilled his glass, guessing he wasn't going to get a

name to put on the register. An extra five thousand might cover the booze these assholes were drinking down.

Regular Joe walked over, pool cue in his hand, leaned on the bar close by Diego, the bumper resting on the floor, Reyes and Billy Wall looking on. "My people ain't going to like you shitting on our deal more than you already did, amigo."

"Deal is you bring guns. I see no guns." Diego shrugged. "I see no deal."

"You're holding coke you already been paid for."

"*Sí.*"

"Got to be one special piece of ass," Joe said, "risk blowing a deal like this."

Diego sipped, looked at Rudi and finally said her name. "Ashika Shakira."

Joe went back to the table, knowing how this would go down with their pres, High Side. Billy Wall racked and took the break, watched the balls roll, nothing dropping down.

"This Ashika . . ." Rudi said to Diego, remembering a headline he read a while back, chick with a name like a pop diva. "She the one stabbed that cop?" Rudi putting it together. "Some gun smuggling thing on the East side, back in the fall."

Diego nodded, reaching in the case, counting out some U.S. bills, sliding the stack to Rudi, saying, "Is five thousand."

Rudi folded the bills, made them disappear, calling Axel from the kitchen, told him to go fetch the woman, all the way from Osoyoos.

"Your shot," Billy said, chalking his cue, watching Rudi and the Mexican.

Joe saying, "Looks like we're getting some badass pussy."

"Could liven things up," Billy said, taking a drink, giving Joe some room.

Calling the six, Joe put it in the corner. Walking around the table, he bumped the Honduran, Reyes spilling beer down his shirt, saying something in Spanish that didn't sound like *how you doing*. Joe turned, taller by half a foot, maybe thirty pounds on this guy with the tats, saying to him, "You want to try that in English, amigo?"

Flicking beer from his shirt, Reyes grinned, hand at his back pocket. Regular Joe turned and lined the next shot, knowing Billy had his back, Billy holding his cue like he might swipe at a piñata.

Joe sank the seven, saying, "Our boy here's gonna teach her to shit in a bucket. Macho dudes needing a woman to run their guns."

Reyes kept the grin, his hand by his pocket.

"Tell you one thing," Joe said. "This boy keeps up the smiley face, I'm going to tap him in his wet spot."

Axel walked to the table, pissed because he just drew the short straw, having to drive all the way out to Osoyoos, the old man telling him to fetch this Hezbollah woman, treating him like the hired help, three fucking hours one way, saying to the bikers, "You fellas play nice — or I got to go to the broom closet?" Where he kept the twelve gauge. Growing up around these guys allowed him to talk like that and still keep his teeth.

Billy saying to him, "You go by your broom closet, boy, how about fetching a couple more of these?" Handing him the empty bottle.

Laughing, Regular Joe bent across the table, messing up

the next shot, scratching on the eight, looking back at the Honduran.

Three beer cans in hand, Axel came back, handing one to Reyes, holding the others out to Regular Joe and Billy. It wasn't lost on them, the bucket-shitter getting served first.

Diego said something in Spanish, Reyes grinning some more at the bikers, following the Mexican out the door.

"Like I said, anytime you want to try that in English, amigo," Joe called to Reyes.

Lining his shot, Billy put one in the corner pocket, guessing he'd have to call High Side, let him know what was going on.

Joe saying he never had pussy off a most-wanted list, drinking his beer, watching Billy take his shot, saying he was sick of these greasers.

Running a rag across the bar, Rudi called over, "Back home, these fellows hack shit with machetes, leave heads on fence posts. Do it just for fun."

"Somebody tell you we knock on doors and sell cookies?" Joe said, studying the table, telling Axel to put on some tunes.

Going to the bar, Axel flipped through a stack of CDs, sticking some ZZ Top into the player, the one with "Jesus Just Left Chicago." Slapping his pocket, making sure he had his keys, he went out the back, bitching about driving to Osoyoos.

Same time, Ramon and Eddie walked in from the dining room side, both stopping at the fireplace, Eddie looking like he wanted to turn and run, Ramon nudging him forward.

Rudi stopped wiping, Joe and Billy looking over. The Mexican with the pomp not with them.

. . . KICKING HOLES IN THE NIGHT

"FUCKER WAS fast, I'll give him that," Ramon said, going for convincing. "Pulls a piece and puts one in Amado, guy reels back and goes over, Eddie shooting Beckman." Ramon sat on the stool, gestured how Eddie drew from the hip, telling it a second time, this time with Diego and Reyes standing there, both looking sour with arms folded, Rudi across the bar, hand by the lead pipe.

"You just standing there holding your dick?" Regular Joe said.

"No, I go jumping in," Ramon said, "'cept Eddie drilled him."

"Eddie, the guy who didn't want to shoot anybody," Billy said.

"Just getting to know him," Eddie threw in. "Wasn't such a bad guy, Amado telling us about his place in Mexico." Looking at Ramon. "Cabo, think it was, am I right?"

"So you're pointing a gun, but this ex-cop pulls and shoots the guy not holding a gun?" Joe asked.

"Yeah, I mean, Beckman shoots him point blank, then

turns on me," Eddie said. "Maybe guessing I didn't have it in me. Guess I showed him different."

"And the girl?"

"No sign of her," Ramon said. "Hey, I mean, we asked, but the guy wasn't exactly cooperating."

"And where's the gun now?"

"Threw it far as I could," Eddie said.

"You *puto*," Diego said, twisting a finger at Eddie. "Should shoot you in head."

"Shit happens, main thing is it got done," Rudi said, lining up shot glasses, saying, "Man goes through something like that, he needs a drink." Filling glasses, he slid them forward, picked one up and toasted, "To . . ."

"Amado," Diego said.

Everyone drank, saying the name, Rudi pouring another round, waiting till everyone downed theirs, then looked at Ramon, saying, "You first, let's see that hand."

"What?"

"Lay it on the bar," Rudi said, tapping a spot in front of him, reaching under the bar, bringing up the pipe.

"What, no, come on . . ."

Regular Joe and Billy grabbed Ramon, forcing the hand down.

"Want you to tell it again," Rudi said, smacking the pipe in his palm, putting on a show for the Mexican. "This time, the way I want to hear it." Giving Ramon a second to think about it.

"It was like we said." Ramon struggling, the bikers holding him, pressing the hand down.

Rudi swung the pipe, crushing bone, shot glasses dancing

on the bar top. Ramon screamed through locked teeth, Joe and Billy letting him go, pushing him out of the way.

Diego and Reyes looked on, captain of the tug twisting away, clutching his arm, growling through the hurt.

"Now you." Rudi said to Eddie.

Eddie tried to bolt, Billy shoving him into Reyes, Reyes shoving him at the bar, Joe grabbing him.

Clutching his hand, Ramon pushed past them, went out the staff-only door, couldn't watch, Billy and Joe pressing Eddie's hand to the bar, Eddie twisting and yelling.

Rudi swung again, Eddie screaming, Rudi doing it twice, Billy and Joe letting go, Eddie slumping to the floor, clutching his hand.

Tossing the pipe under the bar, Rudi looked at Diego, saying, "How we do things."

Diego shrugged, thought the two got off light. He turned and went out the door, Reyes following, saying in Spanish how Ismael would have done it.

Filling his glass, Rudi said to Eddie, "Want to get some ice on it, kid."

Joe and Billy helped Eddie up, sat him on the stool, Joe handing him the glass, saying, "Give you a lift over to Fraser Canyon, have the medics take a look at it."

Eddie in shock, tears rolling down his cheeks, Rudi telling him to drink up, asking, "Know what happens next?"

Eddie shook his head.

"Joe brings you back from the medics, I'm going to ask you again." He refilled the glass. "What you don't want," Rudi said, tapping Eddie's good hand, "is give me the same bullshit twice. Might want to pass that on to Ramon."

Eddie nodded and drank.

Joe motioned for him to follow.

Holding his hand, the pain incredible, Eddie shouldered through the door marked *Authorized Personnel Only*.

The Town Car was right out back, its engine running, Ramon behind the wheel. Eddie coming out the back door and going around the car, Joe stepping to the driver's door, tapping on Ramon's window, telling him to slide over, said he was driving.

Swinging onto the passenger seat, Eddie pulled the door shut, saying, "Told you we should —"

Ramon stared past the dangling rosary, his shirt slick with blood, Joe tapping on Ramon's window. Eddie realizing Ramon was dead, stabbed in the chest. First instinct was to jump out. Then he leaped and punched down Ramon's door lock, doing the same on his side, Joe grabbing the handle, shaking the whole car, yelling at him. Sliding across, Eddie pressed into Ramon. Someone else yelling. More hands grabbing at door handles, fists pounding on the glass. Diego and Reyes trying to get in.

Crowding Ramon, Eddie twisted the key and ground the starter, the engine already running, Joe punching at the window. Throwing it in gear, Eddie jerked the Town Car forward, knocking Reyes away, Diego jumping on the hood, grabbing at the wiper arms, cursing and thumping a fist on the glass, black eyes full of rage.

Tromping his foot down, Eddie gave it gas, wanting to run the Mexican over. Steering with his elbow, he tried reaching Ramon's .357 under the seat. Diego hanging on.

Misjudging the turn on the service road, Eddie bucked the Town Car into the ditch, nose first. The Mexican flew into the reeds. Ramon and Eddie slammed into the wheel, both heads striking the windshield, pain shooting through Eddie's hand. Diego gone from view.

Forcing the door open, Eddie spilled over Ramon, his uncle flopping out into the marsh, head down in the muck. Eddie reached under the seat, grabbed the pistol, leaving Ramon like that, scrambling through the muck and reeds. Not sure where the Mexican landed.

Voices from behind him, running feet. Eddie scrambled around the nose of the Lincoln, knee-deep in the putrid water, feet sticking in the soft bottom, clouds of bugs rising. Moving through the reeds, he made fifty feet before he dropped and listened, ignoring the hurt, knowing what getting caught meant. A lot of yelling going on behind him.

... BETWEEN THE LINES

"WHAT THE fuck?"

Running down the dock, Beck stopped at his empty slip. Then Hattie was at his side, Tilley hat with the ponytail out the back, straw bag in her hand. She put her arms around him, but he shook free, looking at her. "You call the cops?"

"I called you."

"Where's Griff?"

"There were three of them," she said. "Looked like Griff was forced."

Beck tried to calm down, Hattie describing what she saw, told how Griff took the men out.

Had to be the ones he put the flare gun on. Must have looked up his registry, come around and found Griff on board, forced him to take her out. Taking his cell, Beck tried Griff's number, getting voicemail.

Hattie said she already tried, saying they better call the cops now.

Hitting redial, he tried again, the call going straight to voicemail again, Beck hanging up. Crossing the dock, he hopped onto *First Light*, going to her marine radio, his cell ringing in his hand. Checking the display, he answered.

The voice on the line asked him to identify himself. British accent.

"You first, asshole." Had to be the guys that jacked his boat, making demands.

"Still acting the goddamn wally," the voice said. "Shouldn't be a surprise."

"Who the fuck's this?" The voice familiar.

"Hanson, as in Captain John." The accent stuffed with authority.

Beck remembered. "What the fuck you want, Hanson?" Not sure if it was about his boat, or getting towed in last Friday night, the C-Tow guy lodging a complaint.

"Sure that's the best way to start this?"

The two of them had history going back to Beck's rookie days, never took a shine to each other, nearly got into it one night at a cop hangout, enough off-duty guys there to peel them apart. No secret Hanson thought of Beck as more cowboy than cop, too hot-headed for his own good, thinking it got him stabbed on that loading dock, the guy always ignoring procedure. He was glad when Beck took his leave. As far as Hanson was concerned, Beck bought the boat on a pension he hadn't earned.

"Little busy for your bullshit right now, Hanson. You got something to —"

"Calling about a thirty-foot Grady-White, *Triggerfish* across the back?" Hanson read out the ID number.

"She's thirty-two foot, and how about skipping to the part where you tell me where she is?"

The attitude wasn't helping, Hattie nudging him, telling Beck to take it easy and ask about Griff.

Dialing it down, Beck tried again, saying somebody jacked his boat, asking about Griffin Cramb.

"That who ran her up False Creek, doing double the five-knot speed limit?" Hanson said, guessing Beck was back on the bottle, blaming some imaginary friend for his cock-up.

"Where's my boat, Hanson?"

"Waiting with a two-hundred-dollar fine."

"Tell you what, give me your twenty, and I'll come let you cite me personally."

"Right out back of the Granville Market," Hanson said. "Looks like a six-year-old tied her up. That or a lousy drunk."

"Nobody on board?"

"Anybody that was, isn't now."

Beck said he was on his way, throwing in, "Word to the wise, Hanson . . ."

"What's that?"

"Lighten up or call for backup."

"You spend as much time securing your hatches —"

Beck hung up and hurried along the dock, fishing for his keys.

On his heels, Hattie followed him to his Jeep, hand on her hat, clutching her bag, worried about Griff, still telling Beck to calm down.

Going up the steps to the dark parking lot, Beck was first to see the wash of headlights, a Metro cab pulling up, a lime-green hybrid. Getting out the back, Griff stood looking at the two of them, his clothes drooping, wet shirt clinging to his skin, hair matted on his head.

"What the fuck, Griff?" Beck closed the distance.

"Try flagging a ride when you're soaked, middle of the night." Griff backed against the cab, his sneakers squeaking, looking to Hattie.

Beck got in his face, Hattie prying them apart, the cabbie stepping out, saying somebody owed him a fare, Hattie pushing Beck back.

"I owe this guy like fifteen bucks," Griff said, throwing in he got the back seat kind of wet.

Beck dug into one pocket, then the other, turning to Hattie, asking if she had it.

Reaching in her bag for her wallet.

"Hold on," Griff said, remembering the money the guy on the boat gave him, pulling out the soggy bills, peeling off a twenty and handing it across the roof. "Keep it," Griff told the cabbie, the cabbie looking at it, getting in and pulling away. Griff saying, "There were three of them . . ."

Beck folded his arms, waiting.

"Jumped in the drink when the shooting started, lucky I made it to shore. Waves like this . . ."

Beck told Griff to go wait on Hattie's boat, said they'd talk later, going to his Jeep. Following Beck, Hattie told Griff there was a sandwich in the icebox, tea bags in the top drawer.

. . . AFTER LIFE

The Mt. Baker Highway took Ashika Shakira east through the national park. The car in her rearview was far enough back but had been following for several miles going the same speed. Just past a bridge, she pulled off a side road and waited, but the car never passed. Getting dark now, she would have seen the headlights.

Tossing the burner phone off the single-lane bridge, she took the replacement from the glovebox and drove on the main road till full dark, eyes on the rearview, nobody behind her now, finding a spot off a dirt track along the Nooksack River.

Fetal on the passenger seat, she tried to sleep, turning the key to auxiliary, dialing up the heat to fend off the cold, the sound of the babbling water below her. Finally, she drifted off. No idea for how long.

It was a flashlight beam that snapped her awake, a guy in khaki with a big hat, tapping a ring on her window. Her hand went reaching for her bag. First thought, the guy was a park ranger here to tell her there was no overnight parking.

But this guy held a pistol, wagging it, telling her to keep her hands in sight.

Not a park ranger.

Tapping the barrel against the window, he told her to pop the lock. She did like he said. Middle-aged guy, kind of handsome, with a square chin. The kind of guy who had pictures of the grandkids on the mantel. His car was up against her bumper, blocking her in.

"Not an easy gal to find," he said, wagging the pistol again, meaning he wanted her to step out. Marty Schmidt said her name like maybe she didn't know it. Even with the new look, Marty made her, always good with faces. Told her he was with Global Trace. A bounty hunter. Had been dogging her for the better part of a week.

The Bersa was in her purse. Nothing to do but step out.

Marty tugged her arm, standing her up, spinning her to face the car, pressed a knee against her, getting out the flexi-cuffs. Did it like he'd done a hundred times, saying, "Behave and we do this easy, but if you —"

She shot a heel back into his crotch, ringing his bell. Marty folding, wheezing air, dropping the cuffs. Couldn't believe he didn't see that coming. Age slowing him down. Spinning, she drove her knee up, feeling his nose crunch.

Knocked back, ass in the dirt, Marty saw a double image of the woman diving across the front seat, grabbing for her bag. Catching hold of an ankle, he pulled, cursing, blood frothing from his nose. She kicked to break his hold, got her hand in the bag.

Dragging her one-handed, he grabbed for his pistol with his free hand.

Her shot took him high in the chest, firing right through her handbag, Marty getting off a round, putting one through the Accord's headliner. Knocked back down, he was looking like he couldn't believe he'd been hit, trying to raise the pistol.

She stepped out of the car, long legs up over him, knocked his pistol away and said he was too old for this line of work, asked his name again.

He told her, and she said, "Nice meeting you, Marty Schmidt." Ashika firing again.

●

SOMETHING ELSE she couldn't tell the voice on the phone. Dragging the bounty hunter's body behind some scrub, she kicked dirt and tossed branches over him. Rolling his Mini Cooper down a dirt track leading to the river, hidden from the road. Wiping away the tire tracks, Ashika got in the Accord, straightened the wig and kept driving east, ordered the early-bird breakfast at the place called Art's Grill, sitting at the counter like she'd been told: sausage with grits running into her eggs, the coffee bitter, strong and hot.

When only the grits remained, the bell jingled over the door behind her. A stocky man stepped in and sat next to her, daily paper folded under his arm, a heavy smell of aftershave. Catching him in the reflection of the stainless backsplash: a pocked face with a broad nose, a checked shirt and denims. Ordering coffee, black, the man laid his keys and phone down. Never once looked at her. Pressing his weight up, he sighed and headed for the rest room.

The waitress set his coffee down, Ashika waiting and

switching her keys for his, picked up his phone, left enough to cover her tab, something extra for the girl, and headed out the door.

Glancing around, she climbed into the same-color Corolla next to the Honda and backed out. Drove a couple of miles before opening the glovebox. The envelope there held cash and a new map, Ashika heading for the rising sun.

Forty minutes later the big man's cell made a duck-toy tone, the familiar voice telling her to pull off at a place called Omak, said it was marked on her map. An end unit with efficiencies at the Riverside Inn was waiting for her. He hung up.

They were moving her around more, meaning she had some purpose. The room not so bad, its front window facing out to a driveway of grove trees, the main house in view, a shake roof, smoke curling from its chimney. In spite of the country quiet, sleep was fitful the first few nights. The Bersa stayed close. Scrabbling sounds behind the wall panels kept her up, Ashika sharing the place with an infestation of mice.

The Corolla was gone from the parking spot the next morning. Their way of letting her know they were keeping watch. Red tinged the sky to the east, and the scrabbling in the walls stopped. The owner's boy came tapping on the door, leaving a breakfast tray on the step, a tea towel covering it: a bagel, single-serve pack of Smucker's grape, a pad of fresh butter, strips of bacon, nice and crisp, scrambles with fresh-squeezed juice and a carafe of coffee. Drinking the coffee black, she ate and watched the kid play by the main house, riding his scooter around the drive, talking to an invisible friend. Got her thinking about her own daughter, thinking how many years it had been. Fatima would be ten now. She tried recalling her face, the sound of her voice. Tried not to cry.

Tossing the scraps in a corner for the mice, she set the tray outside the door, a handful of change for the kid. She switched on the TV, jiggling the old-school rabbit ears on top. Cable hadn't come to this part of the country, Ashika glad to reconnect with Brooke and Eric and Ridge. Didn't matter about the snow on the screen.

The phone call came on the fourth morning, the voice saying the *Times* ran a story about a bounty hunter killed off the same road she drove down.

"That so?"

He didn't say more about it, told her to get to a place called Tonasket. Some miles north, according to her map. She scribbled a new address, and he hung up. No car mentioned this time.

Putting on the wig and Black Cat shades, she thumbed her way along Route 20. First farmer stopped his faded Dodge, guy named Hank, his pickup bed loaded with cucumbers.

The landscape rolled by, all dried and brown, a contender for the plainest place on Earth, Hank dropping her at the outskirts of Tonasket.

Walking a mile of gravel, she found the rancher, its roof sagging, with a chimney in need of pointing, thistles and crabgrass for a front yard.

Stepping in with the Bersa in her hand, she looked around, then kicked off the ankle boots, found a Frigidaire stocked with Birds Eye, Libby's and Swanson. Stove Top in the pantry, a tin of Green Giant, another of Del Monte, some Folgers and a bottle of soda. An old-school TV and a ratty couch for a bed. This place with cable.

First time in her life she woke to a rooster's crow. Scared the hell out of her. Came close to blowing the beast off the fence rail that first morning, the bird a silhouette against the rising sun, like the one on the Corn Flakes box.

Summer in Tonasket meant the smell of manure coming off the fields, Ashika cooking on the hot plate, the mice in this place bolder than the last, showing themselves, leaving turds and dashing for crumbs. Didn't bother her much.

Halfway through her soaps, she got the call. The same voice telling her they had business. Something they wanted her to do.

Setting on the Revlon wig, looking a long way from the Ashika that topped the most-wanted list, she walked north on the 97, heading back to Canada.

The white-haired guy at the Texaco smiled as she walked up — a woman alone — said he was Chuck, pumping diesel into the Omak seniors' bus, leaning his freckled arm on the pump. She said she'd walked out on her last job in Seattle and decided to just head east, asked about a lift, anyplace away from here. Chuck said he could give her a lift as far as Oroville. Happy for the company.

The gift of the gab, Chuck said he was taking the old girl for fresh gaskets and oil, talked about his missus with the two first names, just won a pie-baking contest, asking if she had a special beau. Told him the last man she got close to, she left with a broken heart. Didn't mention she put a knife in it. Not much luck with men.

Rolling along the 97, Chuck switched the talk to fishing

for smallmouth, the best thing in the world next to a good woman, just relaxing the heck out of life. Said she ought to give it a try. Explaining the characteristics of largemouth and small-, told her what a wobbler was.

Fields, farmhouses and silos. At the *Welcome to Oroville* sign, route 97 called itself Main Street, and Chuck shoved the stick to low gear, the transmission grinding as he shifted. Low buildings, fresh whitewash on the Methodist church, a dancehall of tin siding looking like a hangar, a couple of trailers lining an empty lot. A banner declared a burn ban was in effect, dating back to last fall. The posted speed limit was thirty-five. Across a tilled field another rooster crowed, the only sign of life.

Clicking on his blinker, Chuck pulled up in front of the Main Street Garage, stirring up dust. A dog of mixed ancestry got on its legs and stiff-walked over, its tail wagging.

"That's Rexie," Chuck told her, stepping down and patting the mongrel, pointing her to the Chinese place across the way, place called Lily's Kitchen. "Could do worse than Lily's for grub. Coffee's best in town."

Ashika didn't see anyplace else, asked if he was hungry, her treat.

"Another time maybe." Clapping his stomach on the double helping of his wife's flapjacks, Chuck said, "Woman drowns them with Log Cabin. Never could say no to it."

Saying she couldn't blame him, telling him so long, she crossed the empty two-lane, had the early-bird special at Lily's. The bean-curd cookies in the dish by the cash were dry as crumbs, Ashika washing them down with the takeout coffee. No sign of Chuck at the garage across the road when she stepped out, Rexie lying by the doors, the seniors' bus inside, the tail end sticking out.

Walking the shoulder of the 97, feet killing her in the Burberrys, she kept on till she saw the signs for the duty-free shop up ahead, the border crossing beyond that. Cars lined and waiting. Turning off the road, she skirted an alfalfa field, kept from the farm buildings, crossed more fields and stopped at a stand of trees, hunched against a trunk. She rubbed her feet. They were bleeding in a couple of spots. She ate the last of the bean-curd cookies and caught some rest.

The chill had set in and the sun dropped down by the time she crossed a fallow field, following a tree line, moving through rows of what she guessed was a vineyard, dusk closing around her, the temperature dropping, the cold biting at her.

Back on Canadian soil, she took a side road to the out-skirts of Osoyoos, her teeth chattering. Dark by the time she made town. Signs with arrows pointing out some fast-food joints and a 7-Eleven next to a Petro-Canada.

Going in for a wrapped egg salad, she ate and washed it down with more coffee, the guy behind the register making tourist talk, Ashika warming up, saying she was just visiting friends, waiting for a ride. Then, going around back, she called the number she'd been given, the voice telling her to sit tight. She waited in view of the gas pumps next door, the Dumpster smelling of garbage, offering little shelter from the wind.

. . . SUMMER GIRL

RUBBING HER arms, shivering, Ashika watched cars and trucks pulling to the pumps, people climbing in and out, filling up, swiping their cards, some going inside, then driving off. Nobody paid her any mind.

She didn't go into the 7-Eleven again, couldn't risk drawing attention. Squatting behind the Dumpster, she peed on the blacktop. No tissues in her bag.

The sign at the edge of town boasted that Osoyoos had the warmest welcome. The place was dead. And cold as hell for August, Ashika wondering if Flutie Al-Nabi was hiding in a place like this, her partner running off after she stuck the knife in the cop, the other cop gunning down Baldie Jones behind the Jesus Factory. The papers made it sound righteous, calling it in the line of duty, Ashika hearing the shot that put Baldie down, his hands cuffed. The one she stabbed, Rene Beckman, had a gun in his hand. Gun against knife. She saw the man's eyes again, remembering how she drove the blade, a look like he was surprised. His breath snagged, his body going limp.

Sometimes she wondered if he still saw her eyes like she saw his, wondered if he relived the knife going in. How that felt. She had shot other men — but something about doing it with a knife, it stayed with her.

A red BMW with the top down pulled around the pumps, eased along the side of the 7-Eleven, stupid country music thumping like it had a pulse. The blond kid behind the wheel bopped his head, shades on in spite of it being night, going for a Hollywood look. Had to be Axel Busch, the name she was given.

He watched her get in the passenger side, her hand on the bag.

"Should have come up with a line to say," he said. "You know, some kind of code."

"I know who you are."

"Not a bit like you look in your mug shot, topping Canada's most wanted."

She shut the door, switching off the music.

His smile faded, the woman turning off Johnny Cash, the Man in Black, middle of singing about the beer he had for breakfast. Letting it ride, Axel noted her hand on the bag.

"Guessed you'd have more of an accent," he said, moving the shifter and rolling the Beemer around the pumps, checking his gauge, still had better than half a tank.

"Didn't guess you at all," she said.

He rolled to the exit, told her to snap on her seatbelt, switching the radio back on. Johnny Cash finishing up, Axel saying, "If you want to play with buttons . . ." Pointing. "That one'll put some heat on your seat. Take the chill off."

She settled back, bag in her lap, pressed the seat heater.

"So, you go by Camilla, huh?"

"You know I do."

"You want a coffee or something before we go?"

She shook her head, Axel pulling to the road, slowing for a Camaro of teens whizzing down the main drag, a blonde girl whooping out the top of the sunroof, long hair streaming, the kid driver tromping the pedal, leaving an inch of Daddy's rubber on the asphalt, signs of nightlife in Osoyoos.

"Camilla, yeah, that works," Axel said, pulling into a lane. "Got a kind of Grace Jones thing, the dark skin, but with red hair. Not the way I pictured a terrorist chick would look."

That got a bit of a smile, Ashika looking at this boy playing man in a car his daddy bought, the dark shades, the little beard on his chin moving like wheat in a breeze.

"I'm Axel by the way," he said, offering his hand, still sour about his old man handing him the gopher job. This woman turning out cold as winter.

"Know who you are. How about putting the roof up?" Her hand stayed on her bag.

He slowed, pressed a button and put up the top. Not a bad move considering he was aiding a fugitive. Adjusting his speed, he kept an eye on the rearview, driving the industrial outskirts of town, tapping his fingers on the wheel, Hoyt Axton singing about greenback dollars.

"Don't need your hand on the bag," he said, "'less you're gonna shoot me for playing country."

"I've killed for less," she said, setting her bag on the floor.

Tom T. Hall followed Hoyt, singing about things he loved. Nothing like the Sufi music she grew up with.

Axel kept a check on the rearview, nobody on the highway this time of night. Glancing at her, he said, "Ought to give country a chance. Never know, might grow on you."

. . . LITTLE ON THE SIDE

It woke him. The same dream, Beck on that loading dock behind the Jesus Factory, feeling the knife going in his chest. He remembered those dark eyes.

Beck lay there, listening to the sounds of the marina at night, his body wet with sweat, his heart racing. Told himself he was okay.

Looking over at *First Light*, no light on in Hattie's cabin. His cell was on the ledge, next to the bottle of Johnnie and the pistol. Could call her again, see where it went. The two of them toying with each other since she walked out on Tim the bailiff, guy who worked rent distress. Could ask her to put on the kettle, step across the dock, her drinking tea, him with a scotch. Have a good time.

Should be thinking about the guys who jacked his boat, ones who tried to kill his mate, mistaking him for Beck. Reaching for the bottle, he guessed they'd be back. Do it right the next time. Could call Danny Green, get him to file a report. Taking a drink, he considered his play. The sub would be long gone, but he could look up the tug, pay the captain a visit, get it straightened out. Another drink and his thoughts drifted to Vicki, on board the anti-whaler waiting for a name, pressed tight on Jimmy's bunk. Beck had his shot back in that cove, nearly there. He took another pull, his mind back on her in the raspberry thong. Then he was drifting back to sleep.

. . . FRENCH LEAVE

Thrashing around in the reeds barefoot, his boots back on the gravel by the Town Car, jeans rolled up, Regular Joe was bitching to Billy Wall, saying he should be inside drinking, blaming the Mexican for starting all this shit in the first place. Getting no argument out of Billy.

Rudi came out the back of the lodge, hunting rifle in his hand, telling them to check around the cabins, the cartel guys out front, going up the road, their flashlight beams cutting through the brush. Rudi going close to the old Lincoln, looking at Ramon lying dead and face down. Stabbed by Diego. Wasn't good enough that Rudi smashed his hand with the pipe. The Mexican and his man out there now, hunting the kid.

Eddie stayed low. No way he wanted to end up like Ramon, bleeding out on his cheap vinyl, the Town Car sticking from the ditch a hundred feet from where Eddie hid. Eddie guessing Diego followed his uncle out, stuck the knife in him. Creeping away through the marsh, Eddie made for heavier cover, getting himself close to the line of cabins, cradling his busted hand. Bugs buzzed, drawn by his heat and sweat.

"Where are you, you little fuck?" Regular Joe called, twigs snapping by the marsh, his flashlight sweeping along the drive, shining along the back of the lodge. Billy Wall searched the edge of the marsh north of the Town Car.

If Eddie stayed where he was, they'd find him. Ducking under cedar boughs, he crept through brambles, thorns ripping at him, Eddie careful not to make a sound. Easing toward the last cabin, guessing Rudi would figure he headed for the Crowsnest, making his way to Hope.

Twenty yards between him and Regular Joe, the biker bitching about his bare feet on the gravel, Billy throwing him his boots, Joe stumbling around, stamping his feet into them, walking the drive to the first cabin, clomping around inside, then moving to the next one, Eddie getting as low as he could.

Checking the cabins, two in the middle where the cartel guys were staying, Joe came back along the drive, saying to Billy, "Fucker's halfway to Timbuk-fucking-tu by now."

Rudi made a call, knew a guy with a hound, cradling the rifle, saying to Joe and Billy, "You two take care of that." Meaning Ramon and the car in the ditch.

"You asking or telling?" Joe said.

"Asking. No need telling what happens if that kid makes it to the cops," Rudi said, swinging the barrel across his shoulder. "Fuckers'll be here with their probable cause, and we get nailed with over a ton of shit out back. We're all staring at a lifetime stretch, and you get to explain it to High Side." High Side not known for his gentle nature.

Scuffing his boots in the gravel, Joe turned to Ramon's car, asking, "You got a spot in mind?"

Rudi saying over by the Tunnels, same place they buried the native guy who crossed them a couple of years back, Ramon could keep him company under the trees.

Leaning against the Town Car, Billy pulled out his cell, guessing he better give an update, this whole thing starting to go sideways. Thumbing in High Side's number, getting voicemail. No way he was leaving a message like that. Hanging up, he punched in a second number, hoping he wasn't about to wake Smiling Jack.

. . . EASY ON THE EYES

ASHIKA GLANCED around the cabin where Axel brought her. Told her the lodge and cabins belonged to his family. Not much to this place, quaint in a backwater kind of way. Cleaner than the other places she'd been holing up. No mouse turds that she could see. Kicking off her boots, she sat on the camo bedspread, rubbing her feet.

Axel lingered by the door, saying to her, "You need anything, just got to call up." The phone on the desk was a direct line to the lodge. "Course nobody picks up after nine." Taking the pen and pad, he scratched his cell number, laid it on the desk. "In case you need something after . . ."

"You never know," she said.

Hesitating, then stepping off the porch and crossing to the lodge, he caught a flashlight beam over by the turn in the drive. He walked over. Regular Joe and Billy Wall behind Ramon's Town Car, its ass-end sticking from the ditch, its fender crumpled, driver's door open, reciprocating saw and box of Hefty bags on the ground.

The dead guy flopped from the driver's seat was Ramon,

his head slumped in the ditch. Looking back to the cabin to make sure she was inside, he said, "What the fuck?"

"It ain't good, kid," Joe said. "Not a fucking bit of it." Giving him the short strokes, Joe grabbed the heavy chain, getting on his knees and hooking it around the rear axle, testing it was secure, telling Axel to go get his Beemer to tug this bitch out.

"You kidding me? Use the truck." The off-road ride Joe rigged for smuggling along the muddy back roads.

Billy said he'd get it, Joe flipping him the keys.

Clapping dust from his jeans, Joe picked up the power saw, pointing at the Hefty bags, telling Axel, "Grab a handful. Going to do a little chop-and-drop."

"Fuck me," Axel said. Six hours of driving to Osoyoos and back, now he got to chop up a body, a guy he knew. Not a half-bad guy at that.

Glancing back toward her cabin, guessing there wasn't much she could see from this distance and angle, Axel thinking of the way she said *you never know*. Grabbing bags from the box, he got himself psyched for some blood and fluids.

"Shit happens, kid," Joe said.

Happens a lot around these guys. Axel thinking it, watching Joe power up the DeWalt saw, Axel taking hold of Ramon's leg, glad it wasn't stiff yet, Billy backing the truck along the dirt track.

. . . CLEAN-UP BOYS

HEARD IT. Not sure where it came from, it sounded like a power tool. When it stopped there were distant voices. Middle of the night.

Taking the Bersa, Ashika slipped from bed and padded across the floor, checking the lock on the door, looking out the front window, then tipping the blinds back down.

Going to the bathroom, toes curling on the cold tiles, she laid the pistol on the toilet tank, looking out the small window. Thought she caught some movement near the window, like somebody ducking down. Staring at the spot, she waited, then decided it was nothing but shadows. Then she heard voices again, farther along the drive. Angling the bathroom blinds, she made out a car's silhouette over at the end of the property, the flash of a light.

Two shapes moved around the car. Her guess, some drunk got stuck in a ditch. Nothing to do with her, she got back under the covers, the pistol next to her. Car doors closed, then the sound of a revving engine, the sounds of chains and tires spinning. More voices. Then quiet.

Lying awake — a stupid country song stuck in her head, something about rain coming down and the roof won't hold — she thought of him, the kid telling her it would grow on her. In the dark, she pictured the dumb grin, shades on in the middle of the night, thinking she should have shot his radio. Smiling at the way he hesitated as he walked out the door, saying to her, "You need something after . . ."

. . . BALING OUT

Bits of cedar stuck to his cheek, Eddie swiping them off. Pushing from under the canopy, he moved forward, careful where he stepped.

He could go to the cops, lead them to this place, point them to the bay where the sub lay hidden, sitting in the silt at the bottom end of Gambier Island, its conning tower poking up, branches and debris piled overtop. Ramon had found the spot. Showed them the forgotten road along the south end of Gambier, past the old Christian camp. They could steal back at night and row out from shore, put the guns on board, offload the rest of the blow. Eddie thinking about ratting to the cops, payback for Ramon, might get him immunity, into witness protection.

Sure there was a Greyhound stop in Hope, off of Wallace and Sixth. Guessing it was about a ten-mile hike. Eddie could make it, but Rudi would have people watching for him. Nothing else but provincial parks for miles in any direction. Thirty miles west to Chilliwack.

He heard the rip of the power saw, knowing what it meant. Eddie forcing himself not to throw up, thinking through the screaming pain, why not steal their blow, enough to start over someplace? It was batshit crazy, but they'd be hunting him, looking everywhere but here. And these fuckers owed him plenty. Eddie crossed himself, something he hadn't done in a long time, taking any help he could get.

The coke was hidden out back of the cabins somewhere, Eddie guessing Rudi might have posted a guard. He played it back in his mind, Axel Busch rolling the wheelbarrow behind the cabins. Had to be a shed or a storage unit, likely a path leading right to it. All that blow, Eddie thinking how long since his last line.

Using his good hand, he pushed branches aside, keeping his steps light, feeling his way, moving close to the end cabin. Every few feet, he stopped and listened.

Then he froze. It was a woman's face at the small window. If she saw him he was fucked. He waited. Didn't breathe. Nothing but his heart pounding. Then the blinds tilted shut.

The power saw stopped, and an off-road truck pulled around back. Sounds of them hooking a chain to the Town Car's bumper, snatching the old Lincoln from the ditch. Then it was gone. He crouched, hearing somebody else walking, shoes on gravel, a tap on a door. Then whispers. A woman's voice? He wasn't sure.

Ears straining in the silence, he stayed like that a long time. Nothing but the buzz of insects. When he dared to move again, he went deeper into the cedars, a few feet at a time, getting around the back of the cabin, looking for a shed or something.

Then he heard the snap of a twig and he froze, someone

passing near him, striking a match, the glow of a cigarette, a hand waving out the match. It was Axel Busch.

Moving along a path, Axel exhaled smoke, humming to himself. Eddie following him into the woods, Axel walking into a clearing, unzipping his fly, still humming.

The smell of his tobacco, Eddie staying low, taking his uncle's pistol. Twenty feet between them.

●

BLOWING SMOKE, Axel was thinking of Ashika, his first redhead, a fugitive. Had him by a decade. Undoing his belt before he closed the door. Did it standing. The woman urgent about it. Dragging on the cigarette, he grinned, thinking she might have shot him, Axel tapping on her door after the bikers drove off with Ramon's body in the Hefty bags, Axel left behind, supposed to guard the coke. Planting his feet wide, he unzipped his fly.

●

ZEROING ON the cigarette's glow, Eddie came in low. Axel ground his shoe on the butt, humming, giving a loud exhale as he zipped up, dry leaves crunching underfoot. Eddie raised the pistol and swung, his foot hooking on something, and Eddie went down, landing on his busted hand, crying out.

Mid-zip, Axel jumped, grabbing for his shotgun.

Eddie felt for the pistol, found a stone and scrambled up, pushing away Axel's barrel, catching the side of his head, knocking him into the bush where he'd just pissed. Eddie following him down, a second blow making sure.

Lying there, he was clutching his hand, the pain incredible. Getting his feet under him, picking up the flashlight, he shone it around, found the pistol, found an air vent, then the steel door in the ground, the handle he tripped over, understanding what it was. He switched the light off.

A bunker.

Twisting the handle, he yanked the door up. Dank air rose to greet him. Sticking the flashlight down inside, he switched it back on.

"Fuck me."

He shone the light over at Axel, laid out cold, blood matting his blond hair, fly undone. Staring back into the bunker, Eddie crossed himself again, thanking Jesus Christ, Ramon up there with him. He climbed down the steps.

●

THE BALES were wrapped in heavy plastic. Eddie lifted one by its fabric-tape straps. Shoved it out the door, then two more, then he went back up. Looking at Axel on the ground, he shoved the flashlight into his back pocket, hooked the twelve gauge under his arm, his busted hand hurting, hanging useless. Stacking the bales, he tried to lift. No way. He tried with just two, tossing the shotgun aside. Moving.

Brambles clawed at him, at the plastic, the straps cutting into his wrist. Had to weigh fifty pounds each. Eddie thinking what they were worth, thinking *let it hurt*.

He had to go by the cabin again, past the window where

he saw the woman. No other way to go. Practically holding his breath as he moved down the wall, crossing the drive. At the side of the lodge, he eased the bales down, catching his breath, rewrapping the strap around his good hand. Powder leaking out of one of the bales. Dipping a finger into the tear, he rubbed it across his gums.

Then, peeling off his shirt, he stuffed part of a sleeve into the tear. Wasn't leaving a Hansel-and-Gretel trail, not letting these animals catch him. He felt the rush, thinking the shit was uncut. Eddie riding it, like on the wings of angels. Then he was moving again, knowing Axel would come around anytime, start yelling for help.

Had to get out of there, swipe a car from out front. Shoving the ripped bale with his foot, cradling the other, making his way to the driveway.

A light switched on behind him. Pulling tight to the lodge wall, he glanced back, heart jumping, the light shining from the end cabin. The blinds tipped and the same woman's face looked out. He caught the cinnamon hair, then the light switched off.

Not sure if she saw him this time. Not about to wait and find out. Moving past trash cans, he got to the front, lugging and shoving, letting go of the straps. Nobody out front, the driveway was clear. The torn bale leaking more powder. Eddie getting another taste.

Fruit trees lined the drive, offering little cover, Eddie sliding the bales along the lawn. Thinking of what to do.

The SUV was Rudi's. He tried its doors, then the hatch. All locked. A light blinked on the Range Rover's dash, the alarm armed.

Moonlight on chrome, a bike leaned on its stand, far side of the front door, a Dyna from the look of it. Wouldn't make it far on some one-percenter's ride, juggling two bales of high-grade. Axel's Beemer sat parked halfway down the drive. Carrying one, shoving the other bale with his feet, Eddie got to the car and looked in. Unlocked and no alarm. Opening the door, he felt around under the seat for a spare key. No idea how to bypass the ignition, he yanked at a handful of wires under the steering column, trying to pull them loose, not sure which ones to touch together. Didn't dare switch the flashlight on again.

Somebody called out, and Eddie ducked low behind the door. It came from behind the lodge. He slid both bales down the lawn and into the ditch, the pain shooting up his arm. He kept low, knowing there was no way he could push both bales down the gravel road.

The voice called again, and somewhere a door slammed, then more voices from out back. He took his shirt, putting it back on, dipping his finger in the rip one more time, snorting the powder, leaving that bale. Hoisting the other with his good hand, he started down the road, working through the pain.

Made a hundred yards and had to set it down, gasping for air. More yelling got him moving, lifting the bale off the road, tumbling it into the ditch. He got it up into the trees. Behind him, the sound of the bike firing up.

Getting into the brush, he dropped flat as the Harley roared past, low branches clawing at him. Gathering the bale to him, he scooped leaves and dirt, covering the white plastic.

More yelling back at the lodge, the sound of another engine, a vehicle going the opposite way on the dirt road.

Lying flat on the ground, Eddie listened, putting it together. Nothing he could do but stay down. About ten minutes passed. Shoes sounded on gravel, the Honduran and the Mexican coming along the road, back toward the lodge, flashlights sweeping into the trees, the two of them talking. Couldn't understand their Spanish from this distance, one on either side of the road, sending their beams into the woods, passing the boughs above Eddie.

Maybe fifty feet between them, Eddie held the pistol, made out Diego, guessing it was him who stuck the knife in his uncle, wanting to shoot him. The two men walked back to the lodge.

Eddie watched till their flashlight beams were gone. Sounded like the bike on some nearby road, maybe the Crowsnest. Rolling on his back, Eddie looked up through the branches, saying to the night, "Told you we should run."

If he lived through this night, he'd do things different, sell the coke, clean himself up, live a better life, do it for Ramon.

After a while he rolled to his side and emptied his stomach, then he felt around for a stick. Finding one thick enough, he pressed it against the plastic, trying to poke a small hole, looking up at the night sky, thinking about mirror twins again, like there might be another Ramon out there somewhere, tears rolling down his face.

. . . SCOPING IT

THE COUPLE paddled side by side, one kayak red, the other yellow, going stroke for stroke. Looked like the man would make Salmon Rock ahead of the woman, but not by much.

Easing on the throttle, Beck cruised up the westerly side of Pasley, checking his depth, the cove where they spotted the sub just ahead. Jimmy out on the pulpit, hand shielding his eyes, scanning ahead, watching for deadheads and anything that looked like a conning tower. Jimmy playing like he knew what he was doing.

"Just getting into it when you spotted the sub, huh?" Jimmy called back, shaking his head at the thought.

"Something like that," Beck said, getting that wanting-to-hit-Jimmy feeling again.

"Lucky thing, really, her getting the sub in the shot," Jimmy said. "Out of focus, but still, you can make it out."

How did Jimmy talk him into this? Beck guessed the guy would wet himself if the conning tower rose up right then. Jimmy just playing.

In case it did, Beck had more than a flare pistol this time. The Sig nine millimeter tucked behind the folded chart in the compartment by the throttle, full clip of 124-grain asshole-stopping power. Took the piece off some junkie dealer two years back, its serial number filed down. Never handed it in, Beck kept it, not even sure why. When he quit the force, he stuck it in a drawer and forgot about it.

Pulling into the cove, he made his sweep. Nothing there now but the rotting hull he spotted Friday. Tangles and ferns down to the waterline looked undisturbed. Nobody had stepped ashore.

"Sure this is it, huh?" Jimmy called, coming aft along the rail, Beck using the twin Yamahas, backing her to the mouth.

Glancing at the Lowrance, he cruised to the top end of the island, keeping her a hundred feet from shore, eyes scanning ahead. A merganser perched on a dock rail turned its head, watching them go by.

The wake washed a stony beach, Beck sweeping the west side of Popham Island, then around the rock crop by Little Popham. An offshore breeze was picking up, Beck looking along the logs beached from the last storm. Nothing there.

Took her up to Hermit, Jimmy back on the pulpit, gazing out and playing sailor, Beck at trolling speed down along the east side of Pasley, passing Worlcombe, nothing but a couple of dolphins playing.

Skirting the bottom of Bowen, Beck headed back out into the Strait, cutting taller water, Jimmy making his way back to the console, slipping on his windbreaker. Vancouver Island showed blue in the distance. Clouds massing over its Island Ranges looked like added peaks.

Jimmy, like a broken record, talked some more about saving whales at the bottom of the world, fierce westerlies south of latitude forty, cyclonic storms and crushing sea ice. Telling Beck the waves in the Strait were tame.

Beck tuned him out, remembering *Mañana* was painted on the tug's wheelhouse. Likely find it down at Lonsdale Quay, like a parking lot for tugs down there. Beck pretty sure he could ID the two clowns on board, both with a touch of Latino, one older than the other, maybe related. But they were no threat. It was the ones on the sub, two with shaved heads, heavy on the tats, gang shit. Another one taller, with a wild kind of pomp. The man in charge was the one with the gun, had that Ben Kingsley look, like in *Sexy Beast*.

The way Griff told it: three guys forced him into the Strait, looking to kill him. Fit the description of the guys on the tug, the one with the pomp was from the sub. When the shit went wrong, one guy shot the other, guy with the pomp catching a bullet. Griff bailing over the starboard rail, diving as long as his lungs allowed, freestyling it for his life, making strokes for Spanish Banks, the closest point of land, expecting a bullet in the back.

Could go have a look at the Quay. Find the tug. Could call Danny Green, fill him in on what went down. Beck having a pretty good idea how Danny or anybody from the department would see it: a wild tale of a narco sub in Canadian waters, chalking it up to another ex-cop seeing hundred-proof spooks. Beck known to tip the bottle. The kind of shit that brought laughs around 312 Main.

"Suppose I owe you an apology," Jimmy said, getting his attention. "Knew you had a thing for Vicki, or trying to have one. I should have backed off."

"Girl makes up her own mind," Beck said.

"Yeah, still . . ."

Beck shrugged, the hit-Jimmy feeling fading. If the sub hadn't shown, things would have gone a different way. And he'd have more to show than a raspberry thong. Thinking he should ask Jimmy to return it.

"What's funny?"

"Nothing."

"So, we're cool?" Jimmy said, then stuck out his hand.

"Yeah, we're cool." Beck let go his grip on the wheel, the two of them shaking, both squeezing and smiling. English Bay coming up ahead.

... SLIPPING THROUGH

Must have nodded off, slept through the comedown, felt like something crawling under his shirt, pine needle poking his ear. Moonlight cut through the treetops, Eddie stiff from lying on the ground, the flashlight under him, his hand throbbing with pain, couldn't flex his swollen fingers. Using his good hand, he sat up and shook his shirt, then felt for the bale. No idea how long he had slept.

Only a few hundred yards between him and the lodge. He needed to stash the coke and get out of there. South would take him to the Crowsnest. He needed a car, make his way west to Chilliwack. Figure things out from there.

Swiping dirt and leaves from the plastic, he listened to the night. Getting to his feet, he grabbed the straps, lifted and started, not daring to turn on the light, praying he was moving south, putting distance between him and Rudi's place. Getting his mind off the pain, Eddie tried to imagine some faraway tropical beach, the sun baking him brown, waves lapping the strand, a black-haired woman with a white smile, a flower in her hair.

Crunching twigs and leaves, he stumbled through the thick woods, bumping trees. Still too dark to see much, the stars of no help, his feet hooking stones and roots. Slipping down a gully, a trickle of a runoff, he felt the icy water through his sneakers. Setting the bale down on the bank, he bent and cupped water to his mouth. Stones were slick with moss.

Moving around a deadfall blocking a gully, Eddie guessed he was far enough to chance turning on the flashlight. He pushed the bale up a bank, his shoes slipping, caked with the clay. Sticking his finger in the plastic hole, he was wiping more coke across his gums when he heard it and froze.

Waiting till it came again, Eddie sure it was the baying of a hound. Switching off the light, he was moving, boughs slapping at his face. The pain didn't matter now. Twice more he went down, protecting the hand, grabbing the bale, gauging his direction and moving south.

The baying became louder. No mistaking it. He needed to ditch the bale and get the hell out of there. Nothing but cedar and brambles all around. Pulling on the straps, he dragged the bale across the forest floor, no sense of direction now, just had to keep moving.

He almost ran right into it, a hollowed trunk, a remnant of some long-ago forest fire. The opening big enough to fit the bale. He shoved it in, the baying getting louder.

Through the coke buzz, he heard something else — sounded like an engine. A car driving past, Eddie praying it was the Crowsnest. Just off to his right.

Tossing on handfuls of dirt and leaves, he left the bale and scrambled, moving through the woods, his clothes catching and ripping, Eddie clutching the broken hand to his chest, the baying driving him. Stumbling out on the shoulder of the road, he caught himself from falling, his chest heaving.

The sun was just breaking to the east, Eddie moving west past a marker: *Berkey Creek,* it said, graffiti on the back of the metal sign. Keeping along the shoulder of rock and fern, he tossed away the flashlight, ran and stumbled, the dawn glowing red on a rock outcrop to the north. Best if he stayed to the trees, ducking when he heard a vehicle. Waiting till it passed.

There was a bar in Hope called Skinny's, the guy running the place was Reddit, a guy Eddie scored from once or twice, guy that might help him out. But Rudi Busch would have put out word. Eddie rethinking it, Busch and his boys would know Reddit, too. Best thing was steal a ride and put some miles behind him and here, find a clinic, have someone look at the hand, put down a meal and come back tonight.

There were guys he could talk to at the North Shore shipyards who didn't deal with the bikers, might give him a decent price on the bale. No way he could go back to his apartment for his passport or money. No way he was getting on a WestJet.

Picking a palmful of blackberries, he popped them in his mouth and chewed. Plucking a few more as he kept moving.

Walking until he didn't hear the dogs anymore. Stopping, resting on a rock, checking the hand, brown and purple fingers looking like ballpark franks in the early light, a steady throb of pain running up his arm. Chasing away thoughts of amputation, telling himself he was a good healer. Then another thought came to him: go back to the fishing boat, talk to Beckman, the ex-cop, tell him how it all went down, the jacking of his boat, explain he was as much a victim, show him the hand.

The guy that went over the side had to be crew, Eddie certain he drowned. Good chance the ex-cop wouldn't give him a chance to explain. Still, Rene Beckman would be looking to set things right, being a lawman and all. Eddie might get him to work a deal. Guy had to have cop buddies, right? Guys with flak vests and firepower. Guys that would drool to go bust Rudi Busch and the sub crew, get their hands on a bunker full of blow. If he worked it right, Eddie would square things for Ramon, the assholes getting busted while Eddie slipped away with his bale of coke, enough to set him up for life.

No cars coming on the Crowsnest, Eddie got up and kept moving into the early morning.

. . . BALLING THE JACK

"You want, bunk with us," Jimmy said to Beck, making it sound like he meant it. "You know, play it safe."

Us.

Halfway back across English Bay, Beck eased at the helm of *Triggerfish*, not giving Jimmy anything, wanting to ball up the *WE FUCKED UP EARTH* poster on Jimmy's wall on the anti-whaler and feed it to him.

"I know you can handle yourself, but these guys . . ." Jimmy said.

Beck blew his shot, and Jimmy had moved in. All there was to it. Jimmy and Vicki looking like a couple. Should have left them at the vegan joint, gone back to his boat, kept his date with Hattie, kept *Triggerfish* from getting jacked. Still, wouldn't mind popping Jimmy. Trouble was, once he got started, he'd have trouble stopping. Like, bet you can't hit Jimmy just once.

"What the fuck's so funny?"

Beck shook his head, slowed her into False Creek, easing to starboard, passing a sailboat, an American Betsy Ross flag flapping from its mast. The girls on the deck looked like they'd been painted by Alberto Vargas, the bikinis were tiny and tight, the legs were long and shiny from all that lotion, hands waving boat to boat, the girls in their element, tanning on the deck, the sailboat passing under the girders of the Burrard Bridge, sugar daddy behind the wheel, sporting a trim beard and a captain's cap, flipping Beck a salute.

"Still got pals on the force?" Jimmy asked.

"Few."

"Guys you could tell about the sub?"

"Go in with a story like that . . ." Beck shook his head. "My word with nothing to back it up?"

"You got Vicki's shot."

"One with me naked?"

Seeing what he meant, Jimmy said, "Still, these assholes might come around again."

"Then maybe I'll take care of it."

"Believe you'd try." Going along the rail, Jimmy took up the stern line, Beck throttling down, backing her in, waving over to Hattie on her deck.

Oversized shades and that Tilley hat on, she watched them, her laptop open, teacup on a collapsing table. Lifting the cup, she pointed at something.

"Friend?" Jimmy asked, hopping onto the dock, bending and tying off on a cleat, looking over at her. For a guy with basic training and two tours under his belt, Jimmy was late seeing the big guy five feet away, leaning on the metal light-post, boots on the dock boards, thumbs hooked in his belt loops. Jimmy looked surprised as he came up, the rope in his hands.

"How you doing?" Billy Wall gave him a smile, tats showing below both sleeves, *Pain is temporary* running up on one bicep, *Pride is forever* on the other. Looking at Jimmy, then Beckman, he said, "You fellows know how the natives do it?"

Jimmy kept his eyes on Billy, the guy holding a biker's lid by the strap.

"The way they bag the coho," Billy said.

"We look native to you?" Jimmy said, a couple of feet between them, turning to the side, feet wide apart, Jimmy knowing how to use the distance. Wasn't the first asshole that outweighed him by thirty pounds, Jimmy catching the big ring with the skull, *81* inscribed in its center.

"Way they do it," Billy said, taking his time, "they pile a weir of rocks across the river, shopping carts, whatever. They post a spotter and sit around till he starts yelling. Then everybody runs in, gets wet, bashing fish with sticks, netting them up, kicking them ashore. Call it their ancestral rights."

"Not how we do it," Beck said from the stern.

"Point is," Billy said, looking from one to the other, "it ain't legal, but the law looks the other way."

"You looking for a charter, pal?" Beck said, not needing to see colors to know who this guy was.

"What I'm looking for's answers."

"Then best start asking."

"Few boys I know got on a charter last night. One didn't come back."

"I don't go out past dark," Beck said, standing above Billy on the stern.

Billy taking in the name on the stern, the cartoon fish

and *Coho-a-go-go*. "Drove up in a pile-of-shit Lincoln, old heap with a vinyl roof, something like burgundy." Putting a boot up on Beckman's transom, Billy blocking him from stepping off, guessing he could empty a clip before either of these assholes made a move.

Catching the bulge under the jacket, Beck grinned at the boot. "You want to move it, or you want me to?"

The boot stayed, Billy talking like he hadn't heard him, "Somebody else take her out?"

"Not while I'm breathing."

Catching the woman sitting on the other boat, floppy hat and a drink, Billy eased his foot down, saying, "Maybe I'll check with the lady." He took a step, Jimmy blocking his way, Beck stepping off onto the dock, Billy finding himself flanked.

"Best thing would be leave a number," Beck said. "Case your buddies show."

Billy sized him up. Lucky to still be alive. Looking back at Hattie, he took her for the chick that was with Beckman on the boat Friday evening.

It was the uniform cops coming down the steps from the parking lot, stepping onto the dock, that got Billy smiling and backing off. "Well, thanks for your time, fellas." Clapping Beck's shoulder, he said, "See you around." Billy started walking, thinking he'd swing by the shipyards, check out Ramon's tug. Might find Eddie hiding on board. Take care of him right then and there. Make him tell where he hid the bale, keep it for himself.

Smiling Jack hadn't been smiling last night when Billy made the call, waking him with the news. Fifty more pounds of coke missing and the gun deal gone to hell. The bikers being replaced by some terrorista. The cartel boss wanting to know what happened to their man.

Smiling Jack reamed him out, coming up with a new drop time and meeting spot. Told him he wanted Rudi and Joe to make the run. Told Billy to go find out what happened to the missing Mexican, take care of the asshole with the boat, get some of the East Van brothers to get the rest of their coke off the sub, put the guns on board. When that was done, Smiling Jack wanted Billy to hunt down this Eddie Soto and find the missing bale. Smiling Jack saying somebody better get something fucking right, and hanging up.

Billy and Joe got rid of Ramon's body, then helped the group search for Eddie into the night. Billy going back to his cabin to get a couple hours of sleep, leaving Rudi out there with the hound. He was already gone, making the run to Vancouver by the time Regular Joe and Rudi Busch rolled out just past first light, the fiberglass cap packed with the bales from the bunker, fifty pounds light.

Now he was thinking he'd come back here after dark, bring a chain and roust the ex-cop from his bunk, wrap it around his neck and see if he felt like talking, find out what happened to the greaser.

Angling past the uniforms coming the other way, both young, the chick cop not bad-looking, Billy told them to have a nice day, the cops saying the same.

Danny Green turned, taking a look at the guy, no doubt he was bad news, wondering what the hell Beck was mixed up in.

. . . KNUCKLING DOWN

EDDIE HAD burned the spot into his memory, where he came out on the Crowsnest. The road sign was tagged with graffiti on the back, looked like black scribble. A couple of spindly birch out front of a million pines. Fifty yards into the woods, maybe more.

Telling himself he'd find it again, he moved along the shoulder, staying close to the trees, listening for cars, the throbbing in his hand, Eddie not wanting to look at it. Twice cars approached, Eddie ducking into the trees, waiting till they passed.

He took Exit 173, concrete dividers splitting the lanes, the woods to the north side of the Old Hope Princeton Way, quiet this time of morning. The odd house was set back, no signs of life as he passed.

Rudi would have people looking for him. No way Eddie could chance walking into Hope, wait at the Greyhound stop. A town that size meant everybody knew everybody else's business. Slim chance he'd find a car with the keys in the ignition. He'd have to cut down to the Number One and thumb a ride to Chilliwack, pay for a motel room and get cleaned up, make some calls, see about selling the coke. More chance of finding a car to steal in Chilliwack, weighing his options, come back alone tonight or go to the ex-cop, spark a cop raid, come back then.

Papa Abas was on the south side, a two-story Mediterranean joint calling itself a taverna, a tile roof covered with moss and arched windows, shutters painted blue, gravel parking lot devoid of cars. A *closed* sign hung in the window. The adjoining motel called itself the Knock Knock, its vacancy sign was flashing red. No cars out front there either, just an old aluminum boat in need of paint leaning on the siding, tall grass around it.

He kept moving, a small dog yapping at him from behind a window. An old vw rolled by, brakes squealing as it stopped, an old guy getting out, opening the hatch and dropping a stack of newspapers at the corner, the guy glancing over, giving a wave then driving off, foul exhaust belching from the tailpipe.

A couple hundred yards farther, a light flashed amber at a four-way. The place on the northwest corner was Mickey's RV Ranch. Red neon said the place was open. A half-dozen A- and C-Class boxes on wheels stood lined out front, all late model with white cabs with the same graphics of scenic BC down the sides, Mickey's name over a blue sky, a 1-800 number followed by *mickeys.com*. Sales, rentals and service — explore more, do it in an RV. There were a couple of cars parked around the side; Eddie would check them out, but first things first.

Not wanting to wipe himself with leaves, he risked crossing the lot, thinking he'd ask Mickey for his washroom key. He went in. The guy behind the counter looking up from some paperwork, wild surfer hair and a square jaw, Eddie guessing this was Mickey.

A salesman's smile, Mickey asking, "I help you, son?"

"Can if you got a washroom key," Eddie said.

Mickey's eyes getting clouded with that keys-are-for-customers look.

It was the old man at the end of the counter that turned it around, not looking up from a stack of papers, pen in hand, saying to the surfer, "Hope it's not that kind of place, Mickey."

"How's that?" Mickey asked.

The old guy flipped a page without looking up, saying, "Fellow comes in asking for the restroom, and you turn him away."

"Company policy."

The old guy put the pen down, saying, "As much as I appreciate a man who minds his policy, I got to tell you, I go by principle."

"Not sure I follow," Mickey said, smiling.

"Simply put, this fellow does his business, or I take mine down the road."

Mickey lost the smile, saying, "Come on now, Burt, you're already loaded up, your missus waiting on board. Already swiped your card, plus the closest place is O'Rourke's." Throwing a thumb over his shoulder. "All the way to Chilliwack."

"Easy enough to make a call to AmEx. Top of that, I got all day." Burt looked at him, Mickey put the smile back, looked at Eddie, pointing to the carved horseshoe hanging from a hook on the wall, end of the counter, the word *MEN* routered into the wood, the key dangling from it.

"Appreciate it." Eddie gave the old guy a nod, taking the horseshoe and going around the side. Running cold water over the hand, he stuck it under the dryer, not liking the look of it.

Returning the key to the hook, he thanked the old guy again, on his way back around the side to check the car door locks, the old guy saying he looked like he could use a cup, glancing Mickey's way.

Not sure why, Eddie took the extra stool, found out the old guy was Burt Stone, Burt with a *u*. Looked like one of the grumpy old Muppets, but friendlier.

Signing the rental papers, Burt noticed the hand, Eddie offering it looked worse than it was, saying his beater of a Honda croaked a few miles back, damn hood coming off its prop rod, right down on the hand. A leak in the cooling system. Steam blowing from the rad, a clunking sound coming from deep down.

"Clunking, huh?" Mickey said. "That's never good," gathering the paperwork, checking for Burt's signature. "Should get it tended." Mickey set a paper cup in front of him, asking if he wanted sugar.

"Just cream, thanks." Eddie glanced out the window. Sipping, he found out Burt was picking up one of Mickey's Midi Motorhomes, a Class A with a slide-out room. Eddie asked which way he was heading, Burt telling him the intended route, taking his better half on the road, offering Eddie a lift. Eddie saying anywhere near Chilliwack would be great, taking another glance out the window.

Burt nodded and sipped, didn't ask why he'd go all the way to Chilliwack with a hundred mechanics between here and there. Could see the kid needed medical attention for that hand, Burt knowing there was more, the way Eddie kept looking out the window. Finishing his cup, Burt talked about pulling into the rest stops on the way up to Squamish, check out some Howe Sound sights, maybe Shannon Falls. Booked a chalet in Whistler Village, looked real nice in the brochure, place with a real fireplace, maybe a gondola ride and dinner at Buffalo Bill's. Talked about swinging past Lillooet and Kamloops and following the Number One east, breezing through the mountains, then out to Jasper, spend a night on one of those green lakes, try out the new fly rod.

"Sounds pretty good," Eddie said, guessing Burt for a talker. Sounded more like work to Eddie, steering a rig the size of a pregnant school bus along mountain roads, driving all day.

Finishing his cup, Burt pushed back his chair, asking Eddie, "All set?"

Eddie eager to get out of there.

•

NEVER SAID the wife's name, just called her Puddin', holding the wheel in his crinkled hands. Nicking his head, Burt called over his shoulder, the sleeping compartment behind the curtain. Puddin' didn't answer, Eddie taking a stab the old girl was napping or on some kind of respirator.

Sticking a disc into the player, "A Taste of Honey" by the Tijuana Brass, Burt was saying this baby handled like a dream, and this was the life, how he was glad to shake the old house for a bit, the kids grown, grandkids in school, not seeing much of them apart from holidays. "Isn't that, so?" he called to Puddin' behind the curtain, asked Eddie if he knew about leaving things behind. Eddie saying he had a pretty good idea.

The Trans-Canada rushed by, Burt talking some more about grandkids and how this two-week rental could turn into a purchase, Mickey willing to work a deal. Eddie listening till the *Bridal Falls* sign flashed by, next right. They were closing in on Chilliwack. Eddie still getting used to the idea of Ramon being dead. Cradling the wrist, pushing aside the throbbing pain, Eddie amended his thinking: Puddin' had gone to her reward, up there with her Maker, never heard a peep from behind the curtain. Could be Burt was having a tough time letting the woman go, the pair hitched for half a century. Together long before their hair turned white, skin turned to leather. Eddie had no idea what something like that meant, girls never hanging around for long.

"That reclines," Burt said, meaning the seat, Eddie looking beat.

"I'm good." Eddie saying he had trouble sleeping, blaming lousy dreams, knowing it was on account of all the blow.

"Wait till you get to my age," Burt said, riding the outside lane, the RV rocking in the wheel ruts left by the big rigs.

Eddie was thinking how he'd get word to Uncle DeJesus up in Kent. Let him know about Ramon. Post a letter from someplace on the road. His mind was set: he'd go see Rene Beckman, lay out what happened. A bunker full of blow and a narco sub waiting for a shitload of guns would be enough.

Eddie using the cop raid as a diversion, slip in and grab his stash and get the hell out of there. Drop off the map. The cartel and bikers not about to stamp getting ripped off as "shit happens" and get on with it. Better if they were inside, all doing time.

"What say to tying on the feedbag?" Burt asked, bringing Eddie around, Burt having to repeat it.

"Yeah, guess I could eat." Long time since the fistful of berries.

Burt nicked his head back, calling, "How about you, Puddin', feeling peckish? Got a burger-and-fries place coming up."

●

The Grill 'N Chill sat off the exit ramp. Typical takeout joint of glass and stone. The signage showed a cartoon gopher with *Grilly* on his shirt, running and biting into a burger, looking like he never ate anything so good.

They ate in the rv, Bert Kaempfert doing the "Afrikaan Beat," Eddie putting back a double Grilly with cheddar, squirting a packet of ketchup on his fries. Balling his napkin, he tossed it in the takeout bag, swished Coke around, fryer oil coating the roof of his mouth. Burt polished off his Danish, washing it down with coffee. Nothing for Puddin', Burt explaining in a low voice the old girl was suffering from irritable bowels, blaming free radicals, something about the wrong kind of yeast.

Eddie lowered in his seat, a pair of bikes pulling into the lot, the riders taking a single spot, banner in the window boasting *Grilly's Wing Week*. These weren't Harleys, what

Regular Joe called rice burners. The riders in matching leather stepped off, pulling off full-face helmets, the girl shaking out her hair.

"That's me about a hundred years ago," Burt said, watching the two walk in, helmets tucked under their arms.

"Used to ride?"

"Had an old Indian. Loved that bike." Burt nicked his head at the curtain again. "Love that wasn't shared by all parties concerned."

"I hear you."

"How about you?"

"Me? Ride? No."

"Nothing like the open road." Burt rubbed his spotted hands together, asking, "I interest you in something to finish?" Opening his door, he said he was going for a Chilly-Choc, asking if Eddie ever tried one, chocolate-coated ice cream on a stick, with vanilla flecks, made in heaven.

"How about I get you one?" Eddie said.

"You just sit tight; you're our guest."

Our.

Burt disappearing inside, Eddie considered checking behind the curtain, say how you doing to Puddin'. He let it go, the busted hand looking like it belonged to somebody else, Eddie feeling feverish, wishing he had painkillers, wishing he knew how Ramon would play it, what he'd say about going to see the ex-cop. Thinking about it until Burt shouldered back through the Grill 'N Chill door, a Chilly-Choc in each hand, giving the rice burners another look, shaking his head and grinning.

Taking a Chilly-Choc, Eddie asked, "You mind if I hang in to Vancouver? Maybe drop me at the Grandview exit?"

"What about your car?"

"Got somebody in the city can lend me a hand."

Taking a bite of the chocolate coating, Burt looked at him, Eddie thinking he'd make his way across to False Creek, maybe find a walk-in clinic, lay low till dark, go see Rene Beckman, lay it on the line.

. . . RIGHT THING THE WRONG WAY

"Don't sound so enthused," she said, tucking her bare feet under her, sitting cross-legged on the floor, lettering the sign for HEART, the paint wet and red. Leaning and blowing to dry it, her lips in an O. Wondering what Beck was doing back here, looked like he'd been drinking again.

Leaning against the desk, Beck said no thanks to a cup of Jimmy's coffee, looking at him on his bunk, saying to her, "Got nothing against HEART. Just haven't got your . . ."

"Compassion," Jimmy said.

The urge was coming back, decking Jimmy. Beck saying, "Don't need to go to the South Pole to save the whales, just to . . ."

"Just to what?" she said.

"Forget it."

"What, get in my pants?"

Beck shrugged.

Vicki slapped the brush down, paint blobbing on the floor. "There's a ship that's sailed."

"Reminds me . . ." Reaching in his pocket, Beck pulled

out the raspberry thong and held it out to her, looking at Jimmy. The reason he came down.

After Danny Green came to see him on his boat, catching Beck and Jimmy set to go toe-to-toe with the biker, Beck spent the rest of the day getting to the bottom of a bottle of Johnnie, called Hattie a couple of times, getting no answer. Didn't answer when he went over and knocked on her door, either. The biker didn't show up again, just Griff coming by to ready *Triggerfish* for a charter, making sure the batteries were charged.

Still some left in the bottle when Beck left Griff on board, told him not to fuck anything up this time, Beck driving to the anti-whaler with the last of the Johnnie and the thong, now saying, "Already told you, the Japanese shut down whaling this year."

Vicki snatched the thong from him, tossed it down on the spilled paint.

Jimmy saying there was always Iceland or the Faroes.

Grabbing the brush, she rose, pointing the bristles at Beck, saying, "He tried to help you today, you know that?" Stepping on the thong, grinding a heel, swishing it through the spilled paint. "Know your problem, Beck? You're all about you."

Jimmy sat back, loving the way this was going.

Jamming the brush in the water jar, the water clouding red, Vicki glared at him. Beck went to the door, taking his vibrating phone from his pocket, looking at the text, Vicki stepping behind him, grabbing the door, ready to slam it.

"Shit." He stopped and stared at the screen.

"Piss somebody else off?"

"It's my boat . . ."

And he was running.

. . . SITTING TIGHT

THE VOICE on the phone told her she was going to Mexico, told her how she was getting there. Told her to just sit tight.

Pacing with the Bersa in her hand. Nothing felt right about being in a sub all those days, trapped under the water. Living with mice in the walls was one thing, but Ashika always had a tough time in confined spaces, they took her breath away.

The tap at the door. She nearly sent a round through the wood. Checking the side light, she inched it open, shut it after Axel stepped in.

Stopped him from saying what he wanted. Arms around his neck, kissing him. A stack of towels in his hand, dropping them on the desk, putting his hands on her hips, the two of them getting into it again, Axel backing her to the bed.

The old man and Regular Joe had gone with the coke that morning, six hundred pounds still on the sub, fifty that Eddie stole. With his older brother, Max, up in Pemberton, Rudi told Axel to just sit tight, wait for word on the guns. Billy Wall went to take care of the ex-cop, Diego sitting at the bar, the case with the sat phone next to the bottle, drinking the old man's shit whiskey.

Reyes stood outside her cabin, eyeing Axel when he came out the back door of the lodge, the kid coming with towels this time, middle of the night, holding up a bottle of the same whiskey, saying, "Thought you might be thirsty."

Reyes looked at it, taking the bottle, stepping aside, letting Axel tap on the door.

. . . NITTY GRITTY

THE FLARE gun and a smoldering life-vest laid on the dock. The funk of burnt fiberglass hung in the air. The bow line limp in the water, the edge of the dock charred. He stared at the empty slip.

Hattie slung an arm around him, her eyes wet, the last of the firefighters standing behind her, helmet and all that gear on.

"It's just awful, Beck." She spoke into her fist.

"Where the fuck's Griff?" Left him to watch the boat while he went to see Vicki, dropped off the thong.

She pointed across to *First Light*, putting a hand on his chest, stopping him, saying it happened when Griff took a supper break, went up to the Pirates for buttermilk wings. Hattie promising she'd keep an eye, throwing in, "And he's fine."

He reached down for the Olin flare pistol, shook water from it. This was it, all that was left.

"Want to blame somebody, blame me," she said. "Really am sorry, Beck." Fingers squeezed his shoulder. "And it was me that cut her loose, pushed her out."

Beck needed a drink.

Helmet in hand, the firefighter stepped up like he was offering condolences. Over six feet, weighing in about two-twenty, chiseled jaw.

"Lucky the lady here did what she did, Mr. Beckman," he said. "If the tanks caught, it would have been worse." Pointing to the neighboring boats, the guy talking to him like Beck was six.

"Where is she?" Beck asked.

"Towed her to the launch ramp after we put her out." Pulling off the big glove, he stuck out a big hand. "Dade Holliday, sir."

Hesitating, Beck shook the hand. A probationary firefighter with Fireboat Crew 5, Dade told him, near as they could tell the blaze took place before midnight, preliminaries pointing to it sparking in the galley.

"Arson?" Beck thinking of Griff and that toaster, hoping for something so dumb, but knowing it was the biker from that morning, guy putting his cowboy boot up on the transom. The way the guy said *see you around*.

"No cause yet, sir." Holliday looked from him to her, saying again, "Lucky the lady here called it in, did what she did."

She told Dade to call her Hattie.

The smile was professional, Holliday saying to Beck, "Cut her loose and pushed her out. Quick thinking, you ask me."

"Yeah."

"Kept your neighbors from lighting up," Holliday said. "Family of three were sleeping one boat over."

"The bright side, huh?" Beck said. "It look suspicious to you?"

"Little early for that, but our arson people will take a look."

"Fire just breaks out middle of the night, nobody on board . . ."

"Like I said, little early to say."

Beck regarded the flare in his hand.

"Just be glad nobody got hurt," Holliday said, Beck thinking he used to say shit like that, trying to find a bright spot in the worst kind of hell. His retirement dream up in smoke, and Beck with lapsed insurance.

A couple of uniforms were walking from the parking lot, coming down the steps to the dock. It wasn't Danny Green and Liz Crocker this time. Beck felt their steps on the dock, coming to ask questions, file their report.

"Mrs. Winters, Hattie . . . on behalf of Fireboat Crew 5," Holliday said, holding his hand out, "like to thank you again for your quick action."

Hattie took his hand, wanting to correct him on the Mrs. part. The sixty-pound jacket did little to hide the shoulders — Mr. April in the Hall of Flame calendar, picturing Holliday posing next to a rolled hose with his foot up on it, jacket pulled back to show the abs he worked on between bells — the Colgate smile, the dimpled chin.

Felt like he'd been kicked in the sack, second time tonight, Beck hearing Holliday say again he wished they could have done more.

Hattie thanked him, not sure what to call a firefighter, Holliday telling her just plain Dade would do.

Beck's boat was a total weenie roast, and these two had

sparks flying. The cops coming looked like a pair of rookies, both with notepads at the ready.

Holliday tore himself away, edging by the cops, exchanging professional courtesy.

Jimmy and Vicki were hanging around the edge of the parking lot, insisting they come along after Beck got the call. Pity making them all friends again.

The cops wanted to have a word, Hattie saying to Beck, "Call SeaSmart in the morning. They'll make it right."

Beck watched her go to her boat, Hattie saying over her shoulder, "Tell me you got insurance, Beck?"

"Might have skipped a payment . . ." The envelope had been stuffed in the drawer in the galley, in there with his operator's card, boat license, safety compliance. Never seemed to have the funds when the premiums were due. Living aboard, he didn't worry about it too much. Saw it as wasting money.

Letting go a sigh, she went to make tea, left him to the cops and their notepads, Beck wishing Danny Green had been on shift tonight, taken this call. Wishing he had another bottle of Johnnie Red.

. . . EYE ON THE PRIZE

BILLY WALL kept watch from outside the marina office, the place closed up this time of night, shadows of a maple hiding him. The last firefighter was leaving, two cops walking down the dock to where Beckman was standing with the woman, the woman stepping across the dock to her own boat. Torching Rene Beckman's boat was part of it, getting the ex-cop's attention. Any fingerprint or trace of the Mexican on board was gone now. The cartel wanted the fucker dead, the woman, too, Smiling Jack telling him to get it done. Show the cartel some taking-care-of-business, regain their faith.

Beckman got lucky, hadn't been on board when Billy came the first time. He'd get another chance, catch Beckman with the woman on the other boat, sure she was the one who'd been in the cove. Had a feeling her boat was where Beckman would end up later, the woman looking like the consoling type. Not so happy about it, Billy never did a woman before. Still, it shouldn't be too hard. Slip on board when they were asleep.

He saw Jimmy and Vicki under the light by the steps, recognizing Beckman's smug buddy, guessed Vicki for the buddy's girlfriend. He'd wait till they were gone, then do it quick.

. . . BOUNCING ON THE BOTTOM

THE PAIR of cops headed back up the steps, their notebooks tucked away, going to their cruiser. Beck walked down the dock to where Vicki and Jimmy waited.

"You tell them?" Vicki said.

"What, we spotted a sub? Show them the pic?"

"God, Beck, so you were naked. Get over yourself."

Twenty years of pension with penalty and reduced benefits. Barely enough to secure the loan in the first place, Beck getting the Grady-White by the skin of his teeth, the charters covering the basics with a little left over. Now this.

"Time for a plan B," Jimmy said.

"What you need is to stop pissing people off," Vicki said to Beck, slapping at Jimmy's arm. "Didn't need to go back looking for them."

Beck glanced past Jimmy, Hattie coming along the dock, two mugs in her hand.

"Me, I say we go after them," Jimmy said.

We.

"You for real?" Vicki asked.

"Start with the dickhead put his boot on your boat."

Taking a mug from Hattie, Beck introduced her around, the two women saying hi, Jimmy offering his hand, Hattie asking if anybody else wanted tea.

Nobody did.

Beck needed more than tea, but figured once he got started on the Johnnie Red, he'd wake in back of his Jeep, face in his own puke.

Taking the flare gun from Beck, Jimmy cracked it open, the big shell popping out, dripping water, Jimmy catching it, asking, "We got more than this?"

"Jesus, Jimmy," Vicki said, tugging his sleeve, heading him for the car. "Isn't it bad enough?"

Sipping tea, tasting like it came off a forest floor, mushrooms, pine needles, lichen, Beck watched Vicki saying, "We got whales to save."

"Haven't even agreed on a name yet," Jimmy said, meaning the ship, stepping back to Beck, handing him the flare. "Say we find the biker with the boots. Ask some questions."

Hattie and Vicki looking at them like they were both crazy.

"Can talk to Captain Angus, get my hands on one of the Sea-Doos," Jimmy said, like the girls weren't even there.

"Attack them with a Sea-Doo? What, in our flip-flops?" Beck raising the flare. "And this?"

Hattie hooked Beck's arm, steering him back toward the dock, saying to Vicki, "He's calling his insurance first thing . . . See where he stands, then the refit outfit. Going to be a busy boy." Said good luck with saving whales.

Vicki took Jimmy's hand, telling Beck she was sorry

about the boat, saying to Hattie, "Nice to meet you." Then leading Jimmy to the car, asking if he was nuts.

Beck watched the two heading for Jimmy's car, one of those hybrids, Sea Rangers decal on the door, Jimmy swinging his windbreaker around her shoulders.

"Promised Griff the extra bunk," Hattie said. "But, you want, you can curl up on the deck. Comes with a spare blanket, all the tea you can drink."

"Don't want to be any trouble."

"You can't help that." She saw the silhouette of a man crossing the parking lot, coming from the other way. Nudging Beck.

Beck's first thought it was the asshole with the boots, coming back for more. The figure passed under the lamp, Beck seeing this guy lacked size, coming their way. Recognizing him from the tugboat, he handed Hattie the mug and started forward.

Eddie stopped, knew this was a bad idea, then started to angle away, picking up the pace.

Still parked, Jimmy saw him too, thinking it could be the guy with the matches. Throwing the door open, Jimmy jumped out, forcing the guy to shift direction, Beck grabbing him and spinning him around, getting enough behind the punch, putting Eddie down. Grabbing a fistful of shirt, Beck lifted him back to his feet, knocked him down again, yelling something about his torched boat, Jimmy pulling him off, Hattie running up, yelling, Vicki joining in, Eddie screaming he didn't do it and cradling his busted hand.

Stepping in like a ref, Hattie shoved at Beck, Beck shaking Jimmy off, telling Eddie to start with a name.

"Eddie Soto." Eddie wobbling to his feet, middle of the parking lot.

"The guy on the tug," Beck said.

"Yeah. Other guy on the tug was my uncle." Eddie spilling that they killed him, showing his hand. "Trying to kill me, too."

"Who's *they*?"

"Guys you think I'm with." Getting to his feet and looking around, Eddie's gaze stopped at Vicki, the girl from the boat.

Could be the guy with the boots sent him, setting him up, Beck ready to drag it out of Eddie, send him back with his own message. He said, "You got ten seconds."

Eddie spilled how they moved the blow from the sub to the tug that night, hid the sub, then drove the bales out to Rudi's lodge, how the Mexicans forced him and his uncle back to take care of the witnesses. How they jacked his boat, everything going wrong.

"Who torched her?" Beck asked.

"Don't know that, but take your pick, these guys are all serious crazy. Could be any of them." Eddie told about Ramon getting stabbed to death, how he got away.

Having heard the yelling, Griff came down the dock and up the steps, recognizing Eddie as he came across the lot. Coming at a run, he waded in, windmilling his fists, landing a wild punch, putting Eddie back on the asphalt.

Curling up, Eddie went armadillo, clutching his hand, the skinny guy kicking at him, Beck and Jimmy pulling him off.

Shoving him back, Beck gave Griff a shake, saying, "Can't you see we're talking here?"

Griff pointed. "The fucker who jacked our boat, tried to kill me."

Our boat.

Catching some jacket, Jimmy hauled Eddie up, dusted him off, took hold of the wrist just above the broken hand, putting on some pressure, asking again, who torched the boat.

"Cartel, bikers, take your pick," Eddie said, squirming, telling about the stash in the bunker out back of Rudi Busch's. "All me and Ramon did was run the shit."

"Just got caught in the middle, that it?" Jimmy said, easing his grip.

"Pretty much. Doing it for money."

"And now you want our help?"

"They find me, they'll kill me. Way I see it, we could help each other." Eddie looking at Beck, saying, "Figured you being a cop, me knowing what I know."

"Ex-cop," Hattie said.

"How would that go," Beck asked him, "helping each other?"

"Say I point you to the sub and the lodge."

"Yeah, and you get what?"

"I get even. Take you right to them, the lodge just out past Hope."

Beck thought a moment, asking, "How much you steal?"

Eddie hesitated.

"Their dope, how much?"

"Enough for a new start."

"Enough to get you killed," Hattie said.

"Make a hell of a bust, no?" Eddie asked Beck.

"And how do you see this playing?" Jimmy asked.

"All I know for sure, it's got to be real soon. I can point you to the sub, to the lodge, too."

"And you walk away?"

"I keep what's mine. All I do is point."

Jimmy looked at Beck.

. . . DRAGLINE

FROM BEHIND the maple, Billy Wall didn't get a good look, but he was pretty sure it was Eddie Soto, the kid getting yelled at and bounced around. Billy tucked into the shadows, thinking he had them all in one spot: Beckman, the naked chick and Eddie Soto. Looked like Beckman's buddy from this morning and a couple of others. Could step across and shoot them all right in the parking lot. Thought about it, deciding to wait till the others were gone, catch Beckman alone or with the woman on the other boat, Billy checking the time on his cell.

Digger from the East Van chapter and a new patch were waiting to unload the Chinese guns from the container waiting to pass inspection. They'd load the crates in a van and get them aboard Digger's Boston Whaler. The three of them would make the run up to the bay off Gambier, doing it in the dark, trade the guns for the rest of the coke and get it out to Hope. Billy wanting to give Smiling Jack something to smile about.

Be a bonus if Billy could catch Eddie Soto alone, make him spill where he hid the bale before he killed him.

. . . EDDIE ON ICE

"They got some woman they're smuggling out on the sub," Eddie said. "Taking her back to Mexico."

"Hooker?" Jimmy asked.

"Uh-uhn. Some terrorist chick off the most-wanted list."

Ashika Shakira. Beck felt like the kid just slapped him. Could be a set-up, sending Eddie to lure Beck into an ambush, these guys wanting to finish the job. Beck playing it from all angles.

"Could just go take a look," Jimmy said to him.

"How much you take?" Beck asked Eddie.

"About fifty pounds."

Jimmy whistled.

"Understand, I'm doing this for my uncle," Eddie looked from one to the other. "Guy who raised me, knew me my whole life."

"Stole more than you could carry, and you hid it, likely close to the lodge," Beck said. "Knew I was a cop, figured I'd go storming in —"

"Ex-cop," Hattie said again.

"I go kicking at their door, you go grab your shit. I risk a bullet, and you get rich."

"Not the taking-a-bullet part, but yeah, something like that. I point to the spot, you get the glory."

Could call Danny Green, toss him a bone. Danny calls in the emergency response boys, bags a cartel sub and takes down a hunt camp full of scumbags. Danny moves up the ladder, Beck gains some points back with the department.

"Glory's not going to replace his boat," Jimmy said.

"Look, the shit in the bunker, it's yours. Turn it in, keep it. I don't care."

Beck looked at Jimmy, the wheels were turning, both girls looking pissed, hands on their hips.

"Map's in here." Eddie tapped his temple, knew he had them. "The rest is up to you."

Vicki caught hold of Jimmy's sleeve, saying, "You off your nut?"

Jimmy put his hands on her shoulders, saying, "We're just talking here, babe."

"Want to talk, talk to the cops," Hattie said to Beck, looking at Eddie's hand, telling the kid if he had any brains he'd be on his way to the emergency ward.

"Looks worse than it is, really," Eddie said, waiting on Beck.

"Assholes do owe me a boat," Beck said.

Jimmy nodding.

"What are you gonna do, sell their dope on eBay?" Hattie dashed the rest of the tea at his feet. Turning, she walked back to her boat.

"They love ex-cops in prison, right?" Vicki said.

Beck looked at Jimmy, said, "Let me sleep on it." Turning, he followed Hattie, Griff right behind him.

Eddie saying, "Hey, what about me?"

"You're with me," Jimmy said, thinking he'd find him a bunk on the anti-whaler.

"Don't let him sign you up," Beck said.

Jimmy grinned, asked Eddie what he thought of the name, giving him some options, flipping the keys to the hybrid, Vicki following, Jimmy explaining about the cause, then started talking about sailing to the Southern Ocean, nobody seeing the man in the shadows past the far end of the lot.

. . . DIM, DIM THE LIGHTS

HAULED FROM the water, what remained looked like she had bled out, water draining from the hull, *Triggerfish* up on a trailer, set to one side of the boat ramp. Made Beck feel sick looking at her in the early light. The cabin gutted by flames, the hull charred and blistered, the top gone, the fiberglass pulpit looking limp, the railings blackened and the smell flipping his stomach.

Bought her through a broker, a guy named Paddy Simms, only a hundred and fifty hours on the rebuilt Yamahas. Taking care of the inspection, Simms had her titled, arranged the delivery, had a hand in working the financing. All Beck had to do was get her insured.

Checking the time, thinking Jimmy would be there soon, Beck reconsidered, not sure this was the best way to play it, Hattie giving him royal shit last night, taking his cell from him, looking up the number, making the call for him, telling Danny Green Beck had something to tell him, asked him to come down to her boat, Danny saying he'd be there first thing. Promising to sleep on it, Beck stretched out on her deck, lying awake most of the night, hearing Griff snore down below. Beck sneaking off early.

Now he watched the guy in the Moores suit pull up the knees of his pants, kneeling and placing a filter mask over his nose and mouth, tapping his knuckles against the hull like he was checking for ripeness, duckwalking and twisting his head and looking underneath, a clipboard in his hand, eyes magnified by the lenses of the tortoiseshell frames.

"Who the fuck are you?" Beck said, stopping on the ramp, startling the guy. Seven o'clock in the morning.

Bumping his head on the underside, the guy rose and slipped off his mask, tucked the clipboard under an elbow, swiped at his pants and stuck out his hand. "Malcolm Ross Reid. SeaSmart Refitters. Senior appraiser. Like to get an early start, a jump on the competition." Tugging a card from behind the pens in his shirt pocket, he handed it over, saying, "And you'd be" — read off the form on the clipboard — "Rene Beckman?"

"It's just Beck. Yeah, just meeting somebody down here, thought I'd . . ."

"Say goodbye?"

"Something like that."

Taking a retractable four-color ballpoint from the assortment of pens and pencils sticking up from the pen sleeve in his shirt pocket, going for the red ink, Reid marked an X on his form. "Truly a shame about your boat, Mr. Beck." Saying, while he had him down here, he could use a signature on the form, to speed thing up with the insurance, handing

Beck the pen, clicking it to black ink, adding, "Grady-White makes a fine boat."

"Guess you're going to tell me you can turn her back into one." Beck took the fat pen, clicking it.

Reid looked at him, doubtful, saying, "Anything's possible, Mr. Beck."

Beck looked out to the water, wondering what was taking Jimmy.

Reid pointed to where Beck had to sign, saying, "Form just means you're aware an assessment's being performed," Reid asking who the insurer was, clicking his teeth when Beck told him he might have let that lapse. Then Reid was asking about a home address, Beck telling him *Triggerfish* was it, signing the form.

"Could send the paperwork care of the marina," Reid said, taking it from him, telling Beck he'd be attaching the fire marshal's report to his assessment. Said someone would be in touch in about a week, pointing at the security camera on the dock post. "Shame it wasn't on."

"Way my luck's been running . . ." Beck said, turning. A man stood at the top of the ramp. The guy with the boots.

Billy Wall didn't see Reid at first. He walked to the top of the ramp, grinned, motioning with his thumb for Reid to take off, Reid forgetting Beck had his pen, saying he had what he needed, hurrying up the ramp past the big man, saying his work was done here.

"Hard man to catch alone," Billy said. With Griff onboard *First Light* last night, Billy'd had to wait.

Not at the best vantage, Beck stood lower on the ramp, he dropped the pen and made his move. Ducking under the straight right, Billy sent a hammer into Beck's ribs, pushing Beck back. Folding, Beck threw a shovel hook, not much on it, catching some chin, Billy skipping back a step, shaking it off.

"You the fuck playing with matches?" Beck said, timing the rush.

Billy grinned, his own straight right stopping Beck, Beck sidestepping the follow-up, throwing an uppercut, Billy feinting to the side, landing a hook, blocking and throwing a counter, Beck's nose erupting, blood across his face. Not only big, the guy knew how to box. His moves light despite the boots. Smiling at Beck, saying, "Gonna see your girlfriend right after."

Everything blurred. Sure wasn't going to get it done with his fists, Beck ducked a looping right, scraping his shoe down Billy's shin, catching mostly boot leather. Jimmy and Danny both supposed to meet him down here.

Billy was coming in, leading with a right, his tat flashing *Pain is temporary*. Beck taking the blow, staggering back, a couple more and he'd be done. Another left tagged him and stars shot like fireworks. He stumbled right, the ground coming up. Beck trying to keep his hands up.

Didn't see the boot coming, feeling the spearing in his ribs. He rolled on the ramp, avoiding a stomping. Then his hand found the pen, and he was up, wobbling, took another punch and fell the other way. He started to push up, Billy clutching for Beck's throat from behind, Beck driving the multi-barrel pen in his fist, stabbing it into Billy's thigh. The big man howled, letting go, clutching the leg, blood gushing out. Beck was punching, giving it everything, trying to put the man down, but Billy was limping off. Beck collapsing, rolling on his back, sucking in air.

•

NEXT THING he knew, Jimmy crouched next to him, looking him over, asking if he was alright.

"I look alright to you?" Beck sat up on the boat ramp, spitting blood, assessing the pain, looking around for Billy. "Fucker knows how to throw a punch."

"Guy with the boots?"

Beck nodded. Touching his ribs, hoping nothing was broken, he let Jimmy help him to his feet, seeing Reid at the top of the ramp, saying to him, "Forgot your pen."

"Got a box at the office," Reid saying he called the cops.

Then Danny Green was walking past Reid down the ramp, hands out wide, like what the fuck.

Danny saying he went over to *First Light*, like they agreed. "When a call comes in, a disturbance at the marina office. Just had to be you, right?" Looking at Beck all beat up, blood on his face and his hands, then looking at the mess of a boat. "Still got a knack for making friends, huh?"

"Yeah, a regular people person."

Jimmy grinning, remembering Danny from out front of the Bay, Jimmy now offering his hand.

Danny shook the hand, saying to Beck, "And the naked chick out front of the Bay, you and her . . ."

Beck pointed at Jimmy, said, "She's with him now."

"And the guy who did this . . ." Danny looked at the boat, then at Beck's bloody face. "He her old man?"

"Nothing like that."

"You owe the wrong people money?"

"AmEx is maxed, but so far they just been sending notices."

"So whoever took your boat for a joyride a couple days back, left her out back of the Market . . ."

"Talking to Hanson, huh?"

"Guy likes to talk."

"Guy's a dick."

"And you're not saying squat."

"All I know, somebody took her out, left her tied out back of Granville Market. And last night she got torched."

"So how come I'm down here seven in the morning, looking at you all beat up?"

"Hattie's idea, really."

"The lady on the *First Light*?"

Beck nodded, wiping blood from his mouth with the back of his hand.

Jimmy's phone rang. Taking it out, he turned down the ramp, the Sea-Doo at the edge of the water. He said something, then turned and handed the phone to Beck, saying Vicki wanted a word.

Beck took it, saying, "Don't start."

"Captain Angus's throwing a shindig."

"More vegan cheese?" Beck spitting more blood, Danny checking his pocket for a tissue.

"It's tonight," she said. "A kind of farewell."

"You're really going?"

"We sail in three days, and I want you there. Hattie and Griff, too."

He waited, then said, "I'll be there."

"You call the cops yet?"

"Talking to my old partner right now," he said, taking a tissue from Danny.

"Cop from out front of the Bay?"

"Yeah."

"Tell him to come along, bring his partner and her ticket book." Vicki getting serious, saying, "Want you to keep Jimmy safe."

When he hung up, he wiped with the tissue, looked at Jimmy, saying, "Didn't mention you were sailing off in three days."

"I get a chance?"

"They come up with a name yet?"

"Ship? Yeah, we settled on the SS *Suzuki*. Going to paint on the letters first thing."

Danny interrupted, looking at Beck. "Want to tell me why I'm here?"

It was Billy's ambush that had Beck making up his mind. He looked at Danny, saying, "Want you to come to a party tonight."

. . . DOWN THE BARREL

SEVENTY-FOUR FEET of Kevlar hull. A good craft, in spite of lacking a head. What this thing could use was an attack periscope, a torpedo in a tube. Ismael imagined taking a bearing on some navy boat, setting course, range and speed, angling his bow and hitting the button. Blow the hell out anybody interfering with his business.

Diego was due a bullet, Ismael sure Topo would give him the word. The sub hidden since Friday night and still no word on the guns, Ismael laying the fuck-ups on Diego.

Ismael checked the time — ten minutes later than he was told — and stuck in the battery, switching on the sat phone. It was ringing right away, Diego sounding pissed when he picked up, saying he'd been trying for ten minutes, Ismael saying they should have been gone from here two days ago.

Diego said he didn't need any more of his shit, yelling how he sent Amado after the naked guy, and he ended up dead. Ramon dead, too. Fifty pounds of coke missing. Topo Quintero ordering him to bring a terrorista on board, sneak her back home. He asked Ismael if he got rid of the

Colombian's body. Ismael saying for that he needed deeper water, asking if Diego was trying to spruce up the place on account of the *chica* coming on board. Diego saying again he had enough of his shit, telling him Busch and one of the bikers were taking the coke south of the border, the other biker searching for the naked cop. Saying he was waiting on word about the three hundred guns.

"Who the fuck is in charge?" Ismael asked, and Diego cursed and threatened to shoot him on sight. Ismael laughed and hung up, answering when it rang again, Diego saying he was on his way, told him to be ready.

"Better ask Topo for permission first," Ismael said and made kissing sounds, Diego hanging up this time. Ismael thinking with all Diego's fuck-ups, the cartel boss would be ordering him to tie Diego's hands and feet, chop off the fingers first, then the hands and feet. His manhood. Leave his head on a pike outside his mother's house. It was kinder this way, just shoot him on sight. Then Topo would appoint Ismael captain, put him in charge of the next run.

Ismael was still laughing, going down the rungs. He slit his blade across a corner of one of the bales, inhaled the powder off the knife. Waited for the buzz. Feeling good.

Branches and debris hid the sub tethered to old pilings in water barely deep enough. Stepping over the body, past the box of grenades, Ismael got the twelve-gauge bullpup, sucked more coke up his nose and got something to eat, going back up, setting the pump-action shotgun across his lap, a dual-tube magazine, lining the tins of food on its stock.

Carlos was getting riper by the minute down below. Place could use an air freshener, Ismael laughing as he got his knife out and cut open the tin, thinking about Diego bringing a *terrorista* on board.

His feet dangled down the open hatch, Ismael ate from the tin of Bumble Bee tuna, scooping it with his fingers. A warm can of Dr Pepper forced a belch, watering his eyes. *Americanos* with their food in packages, drinks in cans, their drive-thrus and ice in their urinals. What does any man need to piss on ice for?

The fish in the tin wasn't much, and the Big Stick pepperoni set his chest on fire. It's what Ramon had on the tugboat when they hid the sub, that and a bag of Doritos, all Ismael had to eat since Friday night. Tapping the last one from his pack of Winstons, he lit up, the warning on the side of the pack said smoking would make him impotent. *"Vete a la chingada."* Crushed it in his hand and blew smoke.

Never much for the powder, Ismael went back down the ladder for more after he ate. One time with the death squad he chewed the leaves, somebody saying it would keep him sharp, make him less hungry. *Pura mierda.* He never found it so. Now he did it just to pass the time. Get him crazy enough to kill Diego without waiting for word from Topo. Call it taking initiative. Say Diego went loco and came at him, nothing else he could do.

Lugging dead Carlos, he climbed up the rungs, talking to him, saying it the way he heard it in some film: "Ease good cheet." Repeating the line. "Eats good sheet." Rolling the English, getting his tongue around it. "Good chit. Good shit." His tongue felt numb. The bitter taste of the *cocaína.* The cotton mouth starting. He laid the body down on the hull, arranged some of the cedar branches to hide him.

Leaning back into the boughs, Ismael felt the heat of the sun, talking to the dead man, drawing him an image of the naked man and woman on the boat, *Triggerfish* painted down its hull, two white bodies interrupted in the throes of passion. Laughing at that, saying how Diego decreed the pair had to die. The man making decisions.

Ended up Amado was dead, Ramon was dead, and the naked guy was still alive. The girl, too. And according to Diego, the one called Eddie ran off with fifty pounds. Ismael couldn't stop laughing.

"Diego is a man in deep shit," Ismael said in Spanish, his eyes watering, explaining Lieutenant Topo would not be laughing, Diego getting no sympathy from the cartel boss. Ismael sure to be captain on the next run, throwing a salute at Carlos.

Funny, yes, but Ismael was the one sitting on nearly six hundred pounds of the *cocaína*. If the naked man tipped the authorities, and they came searching, Ismael was fucked. Sitting with his bullpup and a box of grenades, taking all the risks while Diego and Reyes ate hot food and drank whiskey, maybe screwing the terrorista woman.

He eyed a ferry crossing to the south, big and white and the size of a hotel, going from Langdale to Horseshoe Bay. Far enough out, its wake didn't reach to the sub. A water taxi cruised the eastern part of the bay soon after, its hull low in the water, its engine chugging through the morning stillness. Never slowed, never came close.

An eagle floated on currents high above the land, its white head, wings barely moving. High on the powder, Ismael watched the big bird tip its wings on air currents.

Seagulls squawking after the big bird, one getting too close, snatched by the razor talons, an easy meal, the eagle flapping off, holding the seabird like it was nothing. An otter splashed in the kelp bed fifty meters off, the brown fronds lying like lifeless snakes on the surface.

It was the drone of an engine that got him looking through the coke fog, Ismael spotting the Sea-Doo coming into the bay, running along its eastern shore, two figures onboard. Circling the bottom of the island to the western side of the bay, the craft eased to the far side of the kelp bed. The bullpup ready in his hands.

The Sea-Doo approached to within fifty meters, slowed, the two onboard were talking, looked like they stopped to drink water, the one in front passing a bottle back.

Their voices rolled over the water, Ismael not making out the words, both men clad in springsuits, their engine idling. They talked and drank, glanced over at the debris and the old pier. Any closer, it would be an easy shot for the bullpup.

Finger on the trigger, Ismael waited.

Throttling up, the rider veered the machine, slicing the water, heading back to the south, its wake swaying the bull kelp.

Ismael with the bad feeling, setting the bullpup down, watching until the Sea-Doo was nearly out of sight. Climbing the metal rungs, he fetched the sat phone again, came up top and made the call, telling Diego about being spotted, saying Diego better hurry up, telling him to think of what Topo would do. Hanging up. Saying to Carlos it wouldn't be long now.

. . . DOOS AND DON'TS

SLOWING THE Sea-Doo, the waves light at the top end of
Hutt Island, Jimmy checked his fuel, turning to Beck. "You
see it?"

Beck nodded.

Jimmy lifted his goggles, saying, "Should've gone in for
a closer look."

"And get picked off before we're halfway around the
kelp." Beck scooped water into his own goggles.

"Sure you don't want to call in the marines?"

Not going to happen: Beck wanted payback. Plus, he
imagined how the call would go, saying he spotted a narco
sub hiding in a kelp bed. The kind of thing an asshole like
Hanson lived for, seeing Beck lose it to booze. Even Danny
Green would have his doubts, along with the rest of the
department.

"Say we go back when it's dark." Beck betting the sub
would still be there tonight; the crew wouldn't chance
moving it during the day.

. . . OJO POR OJO

Amado never made it back, the *cabrónes* from the tugboat didn't tell it straight. Smashing their hands on the bar didn't bring the truth. Following Ramon out to his car, Diego asked one more time, then used the knife. Felt good doing it. Guy had it coming, embarrassed him in front of his crew.

Not so lucky with the one called Eddie. They searched the roads and the woods, Rudi Busch bringing the hunting dog, searching till daybreak, but Eddie Soto was gone.

It left no choice. They had run the *cocaína* across the border, needed to get the rest off the sub, put the woman on board and disappear, Diego taking his chances, knowing Topo Quintero would blame him if they left the guns behind. Maybe a dead Ismael could take the blame, the other Honduran would say nothing with him gone.

Rudi Busch and Regular Joe had packed up the old truck with eighteen bales and driven off through forest back roads, leaving a dozen out back in the bunker. The younger Busch waiting by the phone for word on the guns, an ice pack clutched to his head where Eddie had clocked him.

Taking the sat phone from the lined box, Diego tried thinking through the booze, considered making another call to Topo, tell him everything was going to plan, say he put Ismael in charge of signaling the craft with the guns, getting them on board, Diego bringing the woman to the sub. Tell Topo they would be underway this very day. He drained his glass, reaching for the bottle, hands wet with sweat.

. . . BLOWING TO BREWSTER

"Fuck me." His head thumped the roof lining again. Felt like taking body blows, Regular Joe feeling it in the kidneys. Bouncing around the passenger seat, the old Blazer humping through another pothole, an old tractor trail in worse shape than Rudi allowed it would be. Detouring around the last deadfall left them both muddy and wet, the Warn winch practically draining the spare battery. The trail snaking across the border, the national forest on the U.S. side, skirting the Conconully. An hour behind schedule.

"Fuckin' shit trail," Regular Joe said, squashing his hat down on his head, smashing his fist on a crane fly on the dash.

"Not hitting them on purpose," Rudi said, fighting the wheel.

The Blazer's body was beat to shit, a modified '92 K5, its rocker panels patched with sealer. Joe put the lift kit under it last spring, dual shocks, extra springs and a skid plate, the light-rack up top, tube-steel bumper with the winch on the front. The bales were stuffed in and strapped down in back, the passenger seat pushed forward, Joe squeezed into the seat.

The Detroit diesel under the hood had slogged the miles of back road, the engine running hot, the gauge needle deep in the red. Rain-filled potholes were the worst Rudi had seen in years, clay packing the treads, the Baja Claws spinning and flinging slop a hundred feet behind the truck, stones slamming the undercarriage. The creek had been a trickle last time he rolled through, now swollen and muddy.

"Better tell Smiling Jack we ran into some shit luck," Rudi said.

Joe got out, slipping in the mud, cursing, looking for a spot to ford. The vp didn't want to hear about more shit luck.

Rudi got out and opened the back, checking the straps holding the bales, didn't like leaving the Mexican back at the lodge with Axel, crazy fucker playing man in charge, drinking too much, wound up too tight.

Staring at the torrent, Joe threw up his arms, cursing at the trees.

The meeting place was a line shack the club had used before, still several miles to the south. A board-and-batten box with a step up to the door, a tiny window and a vent through the tin roof, an old, rotting shitter out back. An overnight spot park rangers once used, forgotten long ago.

Stepping along the bank, slipping and ducking under branches, Joe made his way upstream, looking for the shallowest spot. Thorns raked him.

Rudi stuck in the battery, powered up the sat phone, got the signal, calling the chapter vp, explaining about the washed-out road.

"Trying to call you assholes for the last hour," Smiling Jack said, asking where the fuck Joe was.

"Joe's up the creek," Rudi said, couldn't get another word in, catching a load of shit from Jack. Heard how Tony Boy Bell, the Rocker supposed to be making the meet, got his dumb ass busted an hour back, Smiling Jack telling how the dumb fuck brought his dumb-fuck old lady on the back of his bike, Pam's mouth getting them in deep. Bitch dumber than Tony. Bad enough they had a delay on the three hundred guns. Now this.

Nothing for Rudi to do but let the vp rant till he ran out of steam.

Tony Boy got his ass pulled over at some routine road-side safety check on U.S. 2, a half hour out of Spokane, en route to picking up the prospects making up his crew. "His boys waiting at the cut off for Steamboat Park," Smiling Jack said. "Dumb-fucking-bitch Pam refuses to step off the bike, the cop giving her a warning."

The safety checks had started up after a bounty hunter named Schmidt was found shot to death next to his ride out on the Stevens Pass highway. Rudi remembered reading about it. Only happened about a week back. No leads in the case. Governor's office demanding action — shit like that scared off tourists — and it wasn't happening in his state park. The kind of speech that got votes.

"Bitch tells the trooper to go cavity-search himself," Smiling Jack said.

Holding the phone away, Rudi was looking along the bank, couldn't see Regular Joe now.

"Fucking trooper goes for his piece, and dumb-fuck Tony throttles off, his Fat Boy slinging gravel."

Rudi recalled Tony's sled: black and modified, doing an impressive zero to sixty, hitting a quarter mile in about twelve seconds. Pretty sure his old lady was the one with bad teeth, came into the lodge one night, big mouth on her, trying to get it on with Axel.

"Pam hangs on, whooping, thinking it's funny," Smiling Jack was saying, "Dumb fuck tears along U.S. 2, heading right for Steamboat Park, three hang-arounds left holding their dicks by the ride they just jacked."

Still holding the phone away, Rudi caught sight of Joe coming back, slipping in the torrent, clawing his way up the bank.

"Trooper gets on his mike and puts out the word," Smiling Jack was saying. "Calls his own number and gives chase, bull-bars on his pursuit car."

Rudi held the phone close now, saying yeah, thinking this shit just didn't happen back in Travis Rainey's day.

"Goddamned backups screamed up Tony's ass," Jack went on, "swarm of lights and sirens and the dumb fuck keeps running. Pam chucks a bottle at them. Made ten miles before State Patrol and deputies got their roadblock up, units stretched across the two-lane. Spike strips laid out. Fuckers behind their sunglasses, fingers on triggers, waiting on their sergeant with a bullhorn.

Joe was back, shaking off water, Smiling Jack saying Tony swerved onto the county road and hit the spike strip.

Rudi saying, "Jesus."

"Hit it doing forty. Dumb fucks pitched a hundred feet. Bitch wasn't laughing when she bounced, tell you that much." Smiling Jack saying the probable-cause search turned up an unregistered handgun, open bottle of SoCo, a pill bottle of Oxy in Pam's handbag, fucking fat sarge reading them their rights. Cuffed them to the gurneys, ambulance hauling them away. Tow truck driver clearing the wrecked Harley, handling it like airport luggage. Dumped it on the gravel a couple of times.

"They hurt bad?"

"Want bad? Wait'll I get hold of them," Smiling Jack said, asking if Joe had come back.

"Can't see him," Rudi said, finger to his lips, Joe standing in front of him, dripping water.

"I'm changing the drop spot again," Jack said, told Rudi to get their asses to the fish hatchery over by the Indian Dan Rec Area, the ranger on duty paid to look the other way. "Know where it is?"

"Yeah, I know it," Rudi said.

Tony Boy's smarter brother was making the pickup. Then Smiling Jack hung up. End of conversation.

. . . CINNAMON GIRL

ARMS FOLDED, Diego sat at the bar, hoping he made the right call, getting the sub out of there soon as it got dark, with or without the guns. Coming from the kitchen, Axel repeated what Rudi just told him on the phone, the truck getting stuck in a stream, Rudi and Joe winching her out, the drop-off changed. He put on some tunes, Diego saying it sounded like suffering — *maldito* country and western — a gringo called the Killer crying about his life making a damned good country song. Made no sense. He tossed back the whiskey and poured more.

Twenty-seven million in coke and a biker's woman spits at the cops. "Stupid *gilipollas* in leather," Diego said, against using the bikers from the start. Told Topo they should've used their own people.

Now he was making the call, blame the delay on Ismael, waiting for Topo to pick up the line, Diego starting to speak, Topo saying he already heard it from the Honduran, advising Diego to treat this woman right and keep her safe. Not happy about the delay, Diego telling him the guns were en route, the bikers bringing them to the sub.

"Do not fail again." Then Topo hung up.

Ismael had called Topo first, laying the shit on Diego. Diego would kill the Honduran, then when he got back he'd find Topo's house, bring along some gasoline. Kill his family, too. Make it look like a rival cartel was moving in, sending a message.

Snapping at Axel, he ordered him to go tell the woman to get ready, told him to bring her food, the last decent meal she'd have in many days, showing with his fingers how thick he wanted her meat. He poured more in his glass, the Killer singing about wine spo-dee-o-dee.

"You want to take it easy," Axel said, the Mexican half in the bag, the man in charge looking like he was ready to tip off his stool.

Downing it, feeling the burn, Diego smacked the glass down.

Axel shrugged and went about fixing Ashika a sandwich, bread soft and fresh, slices of turkey, slathered in mayo and grainy mustard, a slice of tomato, an iceberg leaf on top. Sniffing the mayo jar, he spun it around, checking the "best before" date. Guessing it wouldn't kill her.

Three hours together in the car, then Axel tapped on her door middle of the night, telling her he couldn't get her off his mind. Second time he brought her towels, now a sandwich.

Ashika had shut the door behind him that first night, left the lights off and turned it into something, the woman urgent about it. Still thinking about her when he stepped out to the bunker, her smell lingering on his clothes, thinking he might go back for more. That asshole Eddie blindsided him, making off with one of the bales, nobody saying anything, but he could see it in their eyes, they blamed him. The old man hadn't said two words to him since it happened. Didn't give a shit if his head was okay.

Adding a Strub's to the plate now, he picked it up, the Mexican snapping his fingers, wanting to inspect the lunch.

"You serious?" Axel said.

Diego lifted the edge of the bread. Burping, he waved for him to go, told him to turn that shit off.

Snagging a Coke from the ice box, Axel ass-bumped through the door marked *Authorized Personnel Only*, left the music playing.

Reyes was next to inspect the sandwich, the guy playing sentry at her door, the empty whiskey bottle by the wall, Axel pulling the plate away, saying it had been done. Tapping on the door, he waited, telling himself two years of putting up with these guys with the hollow eyes and he'd be set. Have about a million in the bank by then. Never have to do it again.

The door opened, Ashika standing there, Reyes looking on.

"Hope you like turkey with mayo," he said, holding the plate out.

"You make it?" Ashika asked, looking good in the cinnamon hair and tight jeans.

He said yeah, and she nicked her head, meaning for him to come in. Shutting the door on Reyes, she put her back to it.

Axel saying, "That guy could use a personality."

"How's the head?"

"I'll live."

She sat on the bed, the plate in her lap. She bit into the sandwich, nothing delicate about it. Talking around a mouthful, "So someone needs a lift, they send you. Needs towels or a sandwich, you do what you're told." She pulled the zip-top, said his sandwich was good.

"Thanks."

"In my country, a man wouldn't do this." Playing with him, taking another bite.

"Think I'm all the man you can handle."

Got her smiling. "Maybe true. Back home, a man tells the woman, and she just does it. That or she gets hit."

"Can't picture you getting hit."

She smiled, biting into the Strub's.

"Anybody ever do it, hit you?"

"Husband. But only one time."

"You got a husband?"

"Had a husband."

"You left him 'cause he hit you?"

"He died."

"Sorry."

"Shouldn't have hit me." She put the plate beside her on the bed, leaned back on her elbows, patted the spot next to her.

"Remind me not to tick you off," Axel said, getting next to her.

"He liked me to put on tight clothes, took me to discos, for his friends to see."

"Showing you off."

"On the way home one time, we were pulled over, the policeman scolding Amad for the drink on his breath and the Filipina whore in his car, Amad not saying I was his wife, the mother of his child."

"You got a kid?"

"We argued, and at home he drank more and struck me with his fist. When I couldn't get up, he told me to get used to it."

"So you . . ."

"They found him in the lane behind the house; at first, the police said it was over the money in his wallet. A mugging, they called it. Advised me to move with my child to a safer place." She untucked his shirt, working the buttons, Axel looking at the door, Reyes on the other side.

She said sometime later they began to suspect her, Axel asking about her kid again. She put a finger to his lips, didn't want to talk about her life: leaving Fatima with a brother, promising she would be back, taking off with the Somalian who showed her a way out, getting her mixed up with the New Freedom Army, with ties to the Taliban. Supplying guns, bringing them in from Ireland. Scotland Yard seeking her for her part in a London subway bombing two years ago, three people killed, twenty more injured. Fleeing to Tanzania, then Mombasa. The Somalian shot down in a gun battle with peacekeepers. Ashika staying with the freedom fighters, changing her name to Dada Mzungu for a time, Swahili for white sister. Getting mixed up with Flutie Al-Nabi, moved to Montreal, got into running guns through Canada and into the U.S.

She pushed all that out of her head and straddled Axel, touching the bump on his head, asking, "Still hurts?"

"Yeah, it hurts."

She pressed again, and he took her wrists, pinned them down, rolled on top of her, the two of them grinning, finding that rhythm.

•

THE COONS had been back, ones he'd been feeding since the mother paraded her young last spring. Axel swept up eggshells and trash, set a brick on the trash can's lid. Gave him a chance to glance over at her cabin, hoping to catch her at the window. Only time it would happen, is what she said last night. Brought her towels, then the sandwich, and it happened again and again, the tattooed goon outside her door. Still there, looking over at him now.

Checking the time on his cell, Axel went through the door, Diego at the bar, the sat phone pressed to his ear, the bottle on the bar.

Speaking Spanish, sounding agitated on top of drunk. When he hung up, he popped off the back of the phone, snapping out the SIM card. Tossed it on the bar, cursing in Spanish.

Going behind the bar, Axel saw the smashed glass, the sound system on the floor. Diego had thrown his drink at the source of the country music. "What the fuck . . ."

Diego was across the bar, catching him by the throat — another bottle rolling, smashing to the floor — pulling him eye to eye, Axel pushing him off.

Putting a hand to his windpipe, Axel stepped to the

broom closet, reaching in past the shotgun, taking the mop and bucket, gathering up the broken glass, tossing it in the can under the bar, then mopping the spill.

"We go now," was all Diego said, getting off his stool, coming around, helping himself to a fresh bottle of cc from the shelf. One for the road.

"What about the guns?"

"The policeman they say drowned, he is back in life."

"This Rene Beckman guy?"

Pointing at the phone, Diego told him that call was from Ismael, telling him about the two *pendejos* on the Sea-Doo, then told him to get the truck.

The old man's Land Rover. Going to the wall phone in the kitchen, Axel punched in the number for the East Van clubhouse again. Then Billy Wall's cell. Nobody picking up. He tried his old man. Not getting through.

"Fuck . . ." He went back through the swinging door, going in search of Rudi's keys.

. . . GOING FOR TAKEOUT

SOMETHING HE saw on the History Channel, a program about midget subs, two-man Nazi jobs with torpedoes nearly as long as the hull. Getting in close, firing point blank at a convoy's belly, slipping away, and the convoy didn't know what hit them.

The cartels adapted the concept, constructing their subs in the Amazon. Crude as hell at first, not much more than go-fast boats, semi-subs bobbing along the surface with exhaust pipes sticking out of the water. A lot of them didn't make it.

A decade later, they were running two thousand kilometers below the surface, undetected. State of the art and packing tons of blow.

Slave-labor conditions, deadly reptiles, killer mosquitoes. Lugging parts and equipment overland in the Amazon. Subs were built, equipped with radar, sonar, infrared and costing the cartel over a million bucks a pop. A spit in the ocean compared to the net on the powder making its way from Colombia and Ecuador. Stopping in Mexico for a fresh crew and fuel, then non-stop straight up to Vancouver, the DEA and RCMP clueless. Cartels doing whatever they wanted, raking in the dough. That's what Beck put together.

After his RCMP training at Depot, he followed their rules. A rookie thinking he'd make a difference. A year out of basic and that all changed, the street painting him a different picture. Downtown Eastside was nothing but zombie stares and street gangs. Police crackdowns made headlines, but barely made a dent.

Dope coming by the boatloads. Grow-ops and meth labs dotting the Lower Mainland. Pot the reigning cash crop, the hard shit running a tight second.

Kicking in doors and cuffing his share of assholes nearly got him killed. The department not backing him. Beck was happy to leave the life behind, spending his days on the boat, chasing salmon, his skin turning brown. Nothing but the scotch trying to kill him.

Now these guys had torched his boat. Left the flare on the dock, sending a message, making it personal. Just a washed-out cop in the wrong place at the wrong time. Beck sending his own message back, doing it with a pen, giving the sergeant at arms a new limp.

Coal Harbour lay ahead, the green girders of the Lions Gate above. Skirting the top of Stanley Park, lighthouse at Brockton Point and Deadman Island, Jimmy back at the throttle, guiding the Sea-Doo in.

They could just make out the anti-whaler at dock, guys painting over what used to say *RESEARCH* down its white hull, a few more crew members up on deck. Jimmy eased the throttle, steering her to Gasoline Alley's floating station. A tug on its west side, snugged against a line of tire bumpers, two guys in jeans on the deck, filling its massive tank, likely to take hours. Looking over at these two clowns on a Sea-Doo in springsuits and goggles, Jimmy swinging to the far side and tying her off.

"How we doing it?" Jimmy asked.

"Straight on."

Eddie Soto had told it straight. Beck was sure the sub was up there by the kelp bed. Enough daylight left to get the Sig from under the Jeep's seat, grab an extra clip, Jimmy saying he had a piece on board the anti-whaler, souvenir from his last tour. Beck thinking they'd motor back to Gambier and have a closer look, find these fuckers who owed him a boat.

•

NEARLY DUSK by the time they found the spot again, the half-sunken pier with debris around it. Jimmy at the controls, cruising the Sea-Doo around the kelp, came at it from the north end this time, Gambier's long bays like fingers, all in shadow now, greens turning to purple, a couple of blinking lights along the shore of the middle bay.

Jimmy bringing his Ruger, Beck tucking the nine-millimeter Sig in the rear compartment, the Olin flare, crab-trap markers and weights they picked up at the Chevron piled at his feet. Jimmy thinking the markers and weights could tie up the sub's prop. Beck bringing the flare in case he needed to call Danny Green for help, mark the spot.

Scanning from the kelp, neither of them made out the black inflatable shoving out from the rocky shore a hundred yards behind them in the near-dark. Diego, Reyes and

Ashika with a half dozen jerry cans of diesel, enough to get the sub out to the cargo ship *Costas*.

Riding in slow past the kelp, bulbs and fronds bobbing on the surface, Jimmy stood high in front, checking the debris against the waterlogged pier, half its planks missing, looking like broken teeth. Pulling to within thirty yards, Jimmy checked out the jumble sticking above the surface. Pulse pumping.

Same time, Reyes eased the inflatable Seahawk from shore, working the paddles, keeping it quiet, the craft laden with the cans of diesel, the two men on the Sea-Doo facing toward the hidden sub. Diego got in the bow, knife in his hand, the woman in the center, her feet on the cans. The two on the Sea-Doo, the ones Ismael called about, had come back for another look. No sign of police boats. Nobody else around.

Diego slipped over the side. Nothing drunk about him now as he swam.

This was fucked, Axel getting word on the drive out from Hope, Billy Wall and a couple of the East Van bikers on their way, coming by boat with the guns, supposed to be here anytime. Now this . . .

Resting the paddles, Reyes did the same, going over the side, leaving the *terrorista* among the batteries and cans of diesel.

Taking the Bersa from her pack, Ashika kept low, getting in the bow. Easy shot from this distance. Could pick both men off the Sea-Doo, but there was the noise. She would wait, let the Mexican and the one with the tats get it done. The Sea-Doo pulled closer to the sub, both men standing in neoprene vests, nothing that would stop a blade or a bullet, two men about to die.

Resting the pistol on the gunwale, she waited, knowing Axel was watching back along the shore, Ashika facing too many days under the ocean with these smelly men, leaving the boy behind with the Camilla image.

Diego and Reyes bobbed up on either side and just behind the Sea-Doo. Then movement among the debris, Ismael sweeping an arm at some branches, standing over the hatch, his feet spread, dead Carlos spread-eagled on the hull. Swinging the bullpup across his folded arms, Ismael showed the tats, calling to the men on the Sea-Doo, seeing Diego and Reyes swimming up from behind.

"You are the police, *sí*?" Ismael's voice rolled on the water.

Diego and Reyes getting close to the back end.

Jimmy took the flare in one hand, pistol in the other, Beck reaching in the rear compartment, taking his Sig.

"You want to look? Come." Ismael waved, doing his *mi casa es su casa* bit. Showing a lot of teeth, the bullpup across his arms, Diego grabbing for the stern, Reyes on the other side.

Beck held the Sig along his leg, feeling the two men take hold. Reyes grinning up at him, a knife in his hand. Stepping on the fingers, then shoving the bundle of nets and weights with his foot, Beck watched Reyes getting tangled in the nylon line, slashing with the knife, the weights dragging him down, his face fading like a ghost under the surface, air bubbling from his mouth, the markers floating on the surface.

At the same time, the Sea-Doo bobbed, Diego pulling himself up and swinging his own knife. Beck turned enough and fired the Sig. The crack rolling across the water, and Diego was gone.

Beck looked back to Ismael, saying, "Know who I am now?"

"*Sí*, the naked man," Ismael said, this guy saving him the trouble of doing Diego and having to explain it.

"And you people owe me a boat," Beck said.

"Ah, *sí*, you wish it in cash?"

"Cash is king."

"Then come see the king." Ismael bringing the bullpup level, pulling the trigger, Jimmy firing the Ruger and flare at the same time. Jimmy was knocked into the water, Ismael ducked and racked a round, the branches around him catching fire. Beck fired, hitting the periscope. Ismael swatted at the flames, stumbled against the hatch, tripped on dead Carlos, and dropped down into the sub, the bullpup going off.

Deafened by the blast, head striking the metal rungs. Everything black. Ismael thinking he was dead, tasting blood in his mouth. Splayed on the crate of grenades, the wind knocked out of him, a stabbing in his ribs, his ankle felt broken. He felt around for the bullpup.

Flashes of light from out the hatch, the branches burning above him. Sliding off the crate, his breath coming in gasps. Branches burned and crackled, bits dropping around him from above. Spitting blood, he dragged himself for the ladder. Embers fell on the crate of grenades, Ismael kicking it away, trying to scramble up the rungs. The crate catching fire.

●

LAYING THE Sig on the seat, Beck dove after Jimmy, the flames reflecting on the water.

Ismael's shot had taken Jimmy high in the chest, punctured the inflatable behind the Sea-Doo, Ashika jumping from it. The Bersa in her hand, she swam for the Sea-Doo, one man lifting the other onto it. She felt the pain, some of the shot from the bullpup caught her on the shoulder.

She tugged herself up on the Sea-Doo, Beck letting go of Jimmy, reaching for the pistol on the seat. Pointing the Bersa, she smiled, recognizing him, couldn't believe it was the same cop.

The name came to him, Beck saying, "Ashika Shakira."

"Officer Beckman. Nice of you to remember."

"Hard girl to forget." Weighing his chances of grabbing the gun.

"I can help you forget." She pointed the Bersa at him.

"Changed your hair, huh?"

"You like it?" The wig sat twisted on her head.

Branches crumbled, the fire on the sub nearly out. Ismael didn't come back up the hatch. Diego was floating face down. No sign of Reyes. Axel somewhere on the shore, her only token out of here.

The last of the embers dropped, casting them in darkness. She straightened her arm and squeezed the trigger. The roar deafening.

The explosion punched her back, the Sea-Doo tossed, nearly capsized. Felt like a brick slapped his head, Beck was knocked in, he felt himself sinking. Thinking she beat him — again — but he was moving, stroking with his arms, breaking the surface, gasping in air, his ears ringing.

Smoke and stench rolled from the sub's hatch, the hull was gulping in water.

Grabbing for Jimmy, getting his head up, Beck pushed him back up on the Sea-Doo, slumping him over the seat. No idea how bad he was hit. No sign of Ashika now.

The inflatable was gone. Grinding metal over the ringing in his ears, the sub was settling in the muck, starting to list. Beck climbed onto the Sea-Doo and felt for the ignition key, reached Jimmy's jacket for the lanyard clip with the kill-switch, needing to get out of there. Seawater sloshing into the sub's hatch, air gurgling up, debris floating on the surface.

She could swim up on him again. No idea what had happened to her. Beck giving Jimmy mouth-to-mouth, thinking of that knife going through the Kevlar vest, the way it felt back at the Jesus Factory. The front of Jimmy's vest torn away, Jimmy unconscious and in bad shape.

Something floated to the surface. Looked like a head in the Sea-Doo's LED beam. Ashika's red hair. Hearing Jimmy breathing on his own, Beck slid back in, doing a few strokes, and reached to lift her head above water, catching the hair in his fist, flinging it away; in that split second Beck thinking it was her severed head, realizing it was just her wig. He swam back.

Through the ringing in his ears, he heard the *whup whup* of helicopter rotors, searchlight sweeping across the bay, the bird circling from the north. Beck climbed back up, tried to stand, doing his best to wave into the air. Didn't see the Boston Whaler slowing at the top of the bay, switching off its lights. Waiting.

. . . NIGHT ON FIRE

Reyes had lent a hand, pulling the inflatable Seahawk from the tailgate, Axel pumping it up, the two of them lifting the jerry cans from the Range Rover, setting them inside. Axel stood at the shore, Reyes and Diego shoving off, Ashika sitting among the jerry cans. No kiss goodbye. She didn't look back at Axel.

Billy Wall got himself over to the East Van clubhouse after Beck stuck the Bic into his leg, had the fat pen removed by the doc that worked for the club off the books. After the painkillers kicked in, he called up Axel, was told what was happening, they were getting the coke Diego held back off the sub. Billy said the guns were on the Boston Whaler, would meet them at the bottom end of Gambier. Then, he'd go back with Axel, drive the last of the coke out to Rudi's lodge, six hundred pounds of the shit, enough for a few life sentences.

Axel heard it before he saw it, the Sea-Doo buzzing into the bay, its LED light shining past the kelp bed, then switching off. Two riders closing on the hidden sub, Diego paddling the inflatable, slipping over the side, Reyes too, Ashika sitting low among the cans.

Nothing Axel could do but watch it unfold. The flare lit the bay, the gun shots, then the blast from the sub, rocking the night. Scanning across the black water, he called her name.

Axel and Billy Wall were at opposite ends of the bay, both hearing the chopper come with its searchlight sweeping the water.

Billy had Digger switch off his lights, told him to veer off, having to get out of there, the Boston Whaler loaded with guns.

Axel watched it all happen. Then he saw her, crawling to shore, coughing water. Jumping in, he pulled her up on the rocks, the chopper pulling low on the water, one guy on the Sea-Doo waving.

Axel half-carried her through the bush back to Rudi's Range Rover, telling her she'd be alright, thinking of the next move. Driving out of there with the lights off.

. . . HORSESHOES AND HAND GRENADES

"Fucker went up like a meth lab," Beck retelling it, same way he told the detectives: the blast shooting from the hatch, the hull ruptured and bubbling, debris swirling round the conning tower, the narco sub going down. After Jimmy was airlifted to Vancouver General and the detectives asked their questions, Beck called Danny Green. Needed a favor that came without any more questions.

Meeting at the Main Street dock, Danny heard him out. Looking at his ex-partner now, Danny felt a long way from blaming himself for his rookie mistake, the one that nearly got Beck killed. The gym bag with the Hi-Point made them even. Nine mil, black and clean, the bag at Beck's feet. Danny saying he didn't want to know. Glancing at Liz Crocker, his own rookie partner, the two of them acting like they didn't have a thing out of uniform. He reminded Beck, "This woman's nearly killed you twice."

Beck said yeah, the blast of the sub saving him, her bullet whizzing past his ear. Guessing these two were jumping in the sack, he said to Liz, "Should've seen this guy in his rookie day."

"I bet," Liz said, forcing a grin at Danny, liking his old partner, but not liking what Danny was getting mixed up in, glancing at the gym bag.

"You get Betty Crocker when you were a kid?" Beck asked her, trying to keep it light.

"Not a day went by," Liz said. "Kids calling me Easy-Bake. Perfect cake after cake after cake."

"Amazing you still fit the uniform," Danny said. "All that cake."

Putting a hand on her hip, Liz playing. "Got something to say, partner?"

"How the hell you two get any police work done?" Beck said.

She smiled at him, saying, "Caught your pic on the net."

"One with me naked?"

"Thing's going viral. Caption calling you an ex-cop with nothing to hide."

"Yeah, I feel cheap."

"Good parts blacked out, but nothing to be ashamed of from what I could tell," she said, glancing again at the bag. "Any thoughts of making a comeback? On the force, I mean?"

"After the Net thing, likely they'd put me on the Odd Squad."

"You kidding?" Danny said. "You just took a serious bite out of a cartel. Sank their sub and did it with a flare gun."

"And a Sea-Doo and flip-flops," she threw in.

"Just wish I got the bitch," Beck said.

"She's slipped past everybody," Danny said. "csis, fbi, atf, everybody hunting her. Nothing to feel bad about."

"Yeah, but I was this close . . ."

"Shame about the reward though," Danny said.

"Reward?" Beck gave him a dumb look.

"Hundred grand. Just a tip leading to an arrest gets it done."

Picking up the gym bag, Beck was guessing Ashika made it to shore, thinking where could she run.

. . . EASY'S GETTING HARD

HEAD FELT like it was going to explode, Jimmy turned, seeing tubes running from his arm, worst he ever felt. His chest tight under the bandages, a burning in his shoulder, machines beeping with lights blinking.

The nurse told Vicki to keep it short, calling her Mrs. Mosley, telling her Jimmy needed his rest. Vicki pulled the chair next to the bed, taking his hand, her eyes wet when he woke.

"Tell her we're married?" It hurt to talk.

"Only way they were letting me in."

Jimmy tried to smile.

The nurse went past the station; Beck stood reading the board by the elevator, gym bag over his shoulder. Going down the hall, he stepped in, Jimmy in the hospital bed, still getting the girl.

"How's he doing?"

Jimmy looking old, his skin all grey.

"How you think?" she said, looking pissed, telling him he was a true idiot.

Jimmy telling her to lay off.

Beck stood there a moment longer, wanting to say more. He asked if Eddie was still on the anti-whaler, then he turned and went back down the hall, punching the elevator panel, the nurses behind the desk looking his way.

. . . A HYMN AND A HAMMER

FINDING GRIFF asleep in the deck chair, Beck stepped aboard *First Light*, nudged him awake, Hattie sleeping below. Griff looking around at the early light. "Time is it?"

"Payback time." Beck led the way down the dock, telling him Hattie would be fine on her own, the cops promising to send a unit past every hour.

He drove the Jeep to the anti-whaler, the new lettering painted down the sides. Boarding the gangway, clanging on metal steps to the lower level, they found their way to Jimmy's cabin, none of the crew asking what they wanted.

Eddie lay curled on the bunk, his hand properly wrapped, painkillers working wonders, magazine flipped open on the floor.

Beck let the door fly shut. Snatching Eddie by the collar, he pulled him off the bunk, Griff standing by the door.

"Tell me again," Beck said, shaking him. "You at this lodge."

"Okay . . . fuck . . . what . . ." No way to break the hold, Eddie cringed, coming awake in a hurry. "We unloaded the powder like I —"

"Skip to after your hand getting smashed." Beck letting go.

"Like I told you, found my uncle stabbed —"

"Yeah, yeah, in his shit car, then you hid. Stole some blow. After that."

"Right, went out the —"

"Said you saw a woman."

"What? Yeah. In a window. The cabin. Saw her for like a second, but don't think she —"

"Who was she?" Beck shook him.

"Fucked if I know . . . just a face in a window."

"Take it easy, Beck," Griff said, putting a hand on his shoulder. Beck turned to Griff, then eased his grip.

Eddie saying, "Heard the bikers say something about terrorist pussy."

"Yeah."

"One of them wondering if it was any good." Eddie rubbing at his neck. "Was one thing . . ." Eddie said, sitting up.

"Yeah?"

"When Ramon and me came back, the bikers were joking about putting her on the sub, about her having to shit in a bucket. Making fun of Rudi's kid about it, like maybe he'd get a thing going with her."

"How you mean?"

"On account of him having to drive out and fetch her back from Osoyoos, spend all that time with her."

Beck went to the door, looked at Eddie, saying, "You point the way, you can come get your shit."

They were behind Beck going through the door, Eddie clarifying, "I just point to the spot, get my stuff and I walk?"

"You point, then do whatever the fuck you want."

NOT MUCH talk on the drive, Beck stopping in Chilliwack, fueling up, going to the liquor store, then the outlet mall, finding a hardware and a drug store. Getting back in the Jeep, not saying what was in the other bags, he broke the seal on a bottle of scotch, took a pull, offered it around, saying they were going to need it.

Griff took a long drink, passing it back to Eddie, Eddie drinking on top of the codeine sulphate Jimmy took from the ship's med supplies, Jimmy knowing where Captain Angus kept the key. He had grabbed some gauze, too, wrapping Eddie's hand.

Johnnie Red between his thighs, Beck followed the Number One out to the Crowsnest Highway, rolling past Hope, Eddie telling him where to slow, pointing to the spot, the highway marker with the graffiti on the back.

Easing to the gravel shoulder, Beck waited till Eddie climbed out, saying, "You got maybe ten minutes, tops."

Ramon's pistol heavy in his pocket, Eddie shut the door, crossing the westbound lanes.

Griff got back in, Beck pulling onto the asphalt, catching Eddie in the rearview, saying, "Sure, you're up for this?"

"Fuckers tried to kill me, too."

Beck twisted the cap, looking at him, drinking, passing the bottle, the left turn coming up. Took the county road about a half mile in, Beck making another left, the way Eddie told him. Pulling up in the middle of the road, fifty yards to the lodge, Beck took the bottle from Griff, throwing his door open, asking, "You ready?"

Griff nodded yeah.

Beck poured the rest of the scotch out on the road. Reaching the bags on the passenger floor, he took a length of neoprene hose, unscrewed the Jeep's filler cap, stuck in the end of the tube, bent and sucked.

Climbing back in with the scotch bottle full of high octane, Beck looked at Griff, Griff taking the Hi-Point from Beck's gym bag, looking it over.

Reaching an oily rag from under the seat, Beck said, "Know you got to flip the safety off, right?"

"Anytime you want to stop talking like I'm an asshole . . ."

"Guess you're right." Beck stuffed the end of the rag in the bottle.

Griff flipped off the safety. "Think I fucking earned that much."

"Know how this'll go?" Beck said, taking a plastic lighter from the bag.

"Hard." Griff trying to sound like him.

Beck nodded. "We drive up. Anybody comes out —"

"Yeah, I got it, I go *pow pow.*"

"No, I do the *pow pow*ing." Taking the Hi-Point from him, handing over the bottle and lighter, saying, "You're burning the fucker down."

Griff smiled, looking from bottle to lighter. Beck planted his foot on the accelerator, the Jeep slinging gravel.

. . . EYE FOR AN EYE

THE BALE had to be in that burned-out trunk. Life owed him that, Eddie telling himself he was doing this for Ramon.

The ex-cop and his deckhand were taking it to Rudi. Eddie trying not to think what happened if they didn't make it back, knowing Burt Stone wasn't going to roll up in his big RV, save his ass twice, Puddin' behind the curtain.

Crunching on dead leaves, wet ferns slapping against him, he ducked under pine boughs. He stopped, everything looking different in daylight. No baying hounds, the pain killers Jimmy got him wearing off, Eddie taking the pill bottle, popping a couple more.

Swiping at foliage, he pushed through to a clearing, a dry creek bed, a crest beyond it. Moss, ferns and rock. Nothing looking familiar. He dug his fingers in the wet earth, pulling with his good hand, getting some purchase and making his way upslope, knocking stones loose. At the narrow crest, Eddie checked around, nothing looking right.

He slid down the bank, careful he didn't tumble. Muck caking his shoes, wet leaves smelled of mold. He pushed himself up. Moving, then there it was, the burned-out trunk. Going to it, he looked in.

The bale was gone.

Then came the first gunshot. Coming from the lodge.

And Eddie was moving through the trees. Never fired a gun in his life. Ramon's .357 AMT Backup in his pocket.

Past the spot where he slept Saturday night, he stumbled from the woods, coming out at the gravel road. Doing this for Ramon. Eddie going to get what was his.

Passing the mailbox, crossing the lawn, guessing Beck's Jeep was out back, he forgot about the fear, remembering Rudi bringing that pipe down, the old man enjoying himself, his uncle killed by the crazy Mexican, the bikers chopping up the body, Eddie chased by hounds.

Taking out the pistol at the open door, he hardly noticed the place was on fire. Holding it out in front like he'd seen on cop shows, he stepped in, eyes adjusting, flames crackling everywhere, going through the big room, the moose head on fire, the pool table, the bar. The place thick with smoke.

Another shot sounded from out back, above the crackling. Hooking his arm over his nose and mouth, he ducked low through the dining room, coughing past the pool table and trophy heads, everything waiting to burn. Another shot from out back. Elbowing the *Authorized Personnel Only* door, he stepped through and into the galley kitchen.

Crouched by the rear door, Rudi had his back to him, aiming a pistol at the cabin on the end.

"Where's my shit?" Eddie said, lifting his arm.

Rudi Busch turned his head, the little gun in Eddie's left hand, the hand shaking. Turning, he put his pistol on Eddie, betting the kid didn't have the stones.

. . . LITTLE ON THE SIDE

Let her clothes drop to the bathroom floor. Her shoulder burned, starting to feel stiff. The kid got the bleeding to stop, tweezed out the shot, asked her if it hurt. Axel poured on the hydrogen peroxide, put on the Teflon. Did it with an easy touch, like he cared, telling her it was going to be alright, this kid that liked the country music.

When he was done, Ashika let him get on top and they made love again, both lying awake after, Ashika needing a next move. Needing it quick.

Crossing back across the border was her only play. Should have left already, but the kid insisted on driving back here, digging out the shot, dressing the wound. Climbing into the clothes he had given her: a denim shirt, a pair of men's jeans, wide at the waist. Pressing the snaps on the shirt, she rolled the cuffs. She had the Bersa, only a few rounds left.

Axel watched her get dressed, sitting at the desk by the door, his shotgun leaning against the frame, Beemer out in front of the steps.

"We're all set," he said, watching her do up the snaps.

"There's no we," Ashika said, thinking she could make

a call, tell the man on the line what happened, see where it went. Guessing she had become a liability, bad luck had a way of following her. The New Freedom Army would abandon her or come after her. If the kid was with her, they'd kill him, too.

"You ask me," he said, "I'm all you got."

"This will end bad."

"You can save it," Axel said, heard enough of it from the old man when they got back, father and son yelling at each other. Rudi was pissed Axel was risking his neck for this terrorist, bringing her back here. Six hundred pounds of coke still out in the bunker.

"We get in my car and head east, Lethbridge, Moose Jaw. Drive right off the fucking map."

She was thinking south. Cross into Montana, Wyoming, Colorado, New Mexico. Doing it solo. Someone she knew in Las Cruces not connected with the New Freedom Army, drug tunnels she heard about going to Ciudad Juárez. Take it from there.

The sound of crunching gravel got them jumping, Ashika reaching the Bersa off the dresser.

The squeal of brakes.

"Shit." Hoisting the twelve gauge, Axel got next to the window, peeking out, racking the slide, told her to get behind the bed.

Waiting.

Creaking on the planks outside. Axel reached to pull back the door, Beck's kick from the other side, sending it flying in, Axel firing, chunks of door frame flying.

Diving through, under the blast, Beck landed and rolled,

firing up, Axel knocked back and across the bed, Ashika firing at him, then running into the can, slamming and locking the door.

Beck crept around the bed, the kid sliding off, looking at Beck in disbelief, leaving a blood smear on the sheets. Beck kicked the shotgun under the bed.

She fired another round, a jagged hole through the door.

Beck got next to the door, keeping low, hearing movement inside, putting it together. He shouldered the door, looked inside, then he was running out the front.

●

First gunshot had Griff running around back, having thrown the flaming bottle through the lodge's front door. The Beemer in front of the cabin on the end. Beck's Jeep in the middle of the drive, door hanging open. Jumping in, Griff jammed the stick, twisting the key, cranking the engine, intending to swing it around past the line of cabins.

The passenger window burst, and he dropped low, stomping the pedal, grinding the clutch. Not sure he was alive or dead, the thud of bullets puncturing the door, next one ripping into the dash, the windshield blown out.

Rudi stepped from the lodge, pistol held out like it was a turkey shoot, smoke curling behind him, the lodge on fire. He fired into the Jeep, thinking he had the asshole pinned. Reloading, seeing the cabin door open.

It was Beck stepping from the cabin, had him stopping up short.

Beck saying, "Guess you'd be Rudi Busch."

"The ex-cop from the boat," Rudi said, turning to face him. Like some scene from a western.

"Mind if we speed this up?" Beck said. "My reward's getting away."

"You shoot my boy?"

"That him on the floor?" Beck said, holding the pistol down at his side, watching Rudi. "Can't say how bad. You want, I can call it in?"

"I got it."

Working clutch and gas, Griff jerked the Jeep out of the crossfire, rolled to the end of the line of cabins, turning around.

Eyes locked on Beck, Rudi heard the *Authorized Personnel Only* door creaking behind him, above the crackle of fire.

"Where's my shit?" Eddie said and stepped out, one hand bandaged, the other pointing his uncle's gun. Rudi was flanked with Beck on the cabin steps, the kid behind him. Turning as he dove, bringing his pistol up.

Eddie fired.

Rudi felt like he'd been kicked, the kid standing over him, asking again.

Blood staining his shirt, Rudi said, "You're a little fuck —"

And Eddie fired again, then emptied the clip, as Beck was moving past the Beemer, around the back of the cabin, eyes sharp, finding the trail.

•

STARING UP like he couldn't believe it — hit five times in the chest — Rudi tried to speak.

Bending, Eddie held up the wrapped hand, fingers poking out the end, bruised and swollen. He tried flipping the old man the bird, his busted fingers not moving right, asking again where his shit was, but the old man was gone.

Griff rolled up in the Jeep, saying, "Should've waited for the answer, then shot him."

"Yeah, hindsight's a bitch." Eddie was moving, telling Griff to keep her running, hurrying around the cabin, same way Beck had gone.

●

AT THE back corner of the cabin, Beck looked out, then moved, staying low, picking up the trail to the clearing. Down in a crouch. Listening. Looking around. Telling himself not to hesitate. If he got his chance, he'd put a bullet in her. Didn't matter she was a woman.

A pair of wheelbarrows were piled upside down at the edge of the clearing. Then he saw it, the steel door in the ground, knowing what it was. Getting low, he crouched behind it so he could use the door like a shield, pull it up a few inches, take a look.

Eddie hurried down the path, branches slapping as he ran, pistol in hand, seeing Beck in the clearing with the bunker's handle in his hand. Pistol aimed at the ground, Eddie told him to back away, adding, "Please."

Beck looked at him.

"My shit's in there." The pistol shaking in his hand.

Beck shrugged and shifted to the side, pulling the door open a few inches.

Ashika fired a round from below, hitting the steel door, the bullet ricocheting back inside the bunker, Beck dropping the door back down, Eddie getting the point.

"Fuck me." Eddie dropped the pistol.

Beck slipped his piece in his pocket, went and tipped up the barrows, told Eddie how this would go, the two of them filling the barrows with stones they found in the clearing, Beck parking them on the door.

Ashika called out, wanting to make a deal, trade the coke for her freedom, pounding with her fists.

Eddie saying there was enough blow down there to make them all crazy rich. Beck thought about it, picked up Eddie's gun, made sure it was empty, handed it to him, then he pulled his cell and punched in a number, getting a signal, saying, "Hey Danny, how much you say that reward was?"

•

GRIFF WAS waiting when they came around the side of the cabin, Eddie still arguing about leaving the coke, Beck reminding Eddie he got to shoot the guy who killed his uncle, smashed his hand.

Eddie tucked his pistol in his belt, shaking his head, looking over at Rudi, wanting to shoot him some more.

Flames showed at every window of the lodge now, the heat intense, the air thick with smoke.

Griff threw a thumb, motioned for them to get into the Jeep, asking, "What about him?" Looking at Axel's boot sticking from the cabin door.

Beck said he wasn't going anywhere.

"Fuck him," Eddie said, pushing the seat up, climbing in back. Bastard helped cut up his uncle.

Beck got in, Griff rolling away from the burning lodge, flames sweeping up the exterior boards.

Griff drove out on the county road, got on the Crowsnest, the smoke rising over the treetops behind them.

Thinking about running the *Mañana* on his own, Eddie said, "Fuckers on the sub shit in a bucket, you know that?"

"That right?"

"Whole crew and one bucket. Hard to imagine."

Engine 1 and the command truck passed them, racing the other way, a couple of RCMP cruisers right behind them, all screaming past with lights flashing. Another fire truck racing toward them before they got past Hope.

. . . ROARING FORTIES AND FURIOUS FIFTIES

ROARING, FURIOUS and screaming: three latitudes of hell. Two hundred and fifty tons of steel, fifty-six meters long. The SS *Suzuki* pulled from port, Canadian flag flapping. Grey skies and frozen seas waiting to toss them in southern squalls, waves as tall as buildings.

Beck stood between Griff and Jimmy on the dock, Jimmy's arm in a sling. The three of them watching the crew hustling, casting off. The word *RESEARCH* had been painted over, the paint still drying. They waved, Vicki waving back from the upper rail, Nemo and Knut standing with her, all in *ANTARCTIC CREW* T-shirts.

"Gonna miss her?" Beck asked.

"Girl's got whales to save," Jimmy said.

"Told you the Japanese cut out whaling," Beck said.

Jimmy just grinned.

Captain Angus sounded the horn, a garbled announcement over the ship's PA.

"Be austral summer by the time they make it down," Jimmy said. "Minkes'll be migrating, feeding mainly on krill."

"That's vegetarian, right?" Griff said.

"It's what whales eat," Jimmy said. "A kind of a shrimp."

Beck turned, thinking of the reward coming his way, Ashika Shakira worth a hundred grand. Thinking he'd cut Eddie in for a piece. Then there was Jimmy and Griff. The Jeep sat out on Waterfront by the Helijet place, shot to hell with the windows blown out, Jimmy and Griff following him.

Vicki promised to post shots of her doing the polar bear swim — the chick crazy enough to do it, leap off the deck into Antarctic waters, Beck betting she did it in a thong. Sure to end up all over the internet.

"How about we get something to eat? I'm starved," Griff said, going to the passenger side, Jimmy hobbling behind.

Beck said he was driving by Hattie's, get her to put on some tea, take care of some unfinished business.

"Oh, nearly forgot . . ." Griff said, digging in a pocket, pulling up a pair of keys twist-tied together. "Told me to tell you, she's off to Pismo Beach."

"Hattie?" Beck caught the keys, *First Light* written on the tag, with a little ink heart.

"Yeah, she left this morning. Her and her ex patching things up."

"Pismo, huh?"

"Said they'd be back before the springs run."

Beck regarded the keys, thinking he'd stop off for a bottle.

"Said you can pay her rent, case you feel weird about using her boat."

Beck pocketed the keys. "Guess we're back in business."

"You're in business. Me, I'm giving my notice."

"Doing it now?"

"Going to work for Eddie, on the tug, learn about hauling logs."

Beck just looked at him, finally put out his hand. Griff grinned, shaking his hand.

"What say to a Sloppy Jane, boys?" Jimmy said. "On me. Celebrate with Griff. Give Beck a chance to get to know his new deckhand." Jimmy pointing a thumb at himself.

"You?"

"Least you can do, right?"

Beck grinned, thinking he might just hit Jimmy yet, Griff asking what the hell a Sloppy Jane was.

"You'll love 'em, kid," Jimmy was saying, describing what went into one, looking at the Jeep: bullet hole in the door, another through the dash, the windshield and passenger window gone.

Beck waited for Griff to get in back, Jimmy taking his time, the pain slowing him down. Pulling himself onto the passenger seat, he shut the door. Then Beck pulled away, he and Jimmy looking between the buildings, out at the big ship.

ACKNOWLEDGMENTS

THANK YOU to my publisher Jack David, and to Crissy Calhoun, Erin Creasey, Jenna Illies, Rachel Ironstone and everyone at ECW. As always, it's been great working with my editor Emily Schultz. Also, thanks goes to copy editor Peter Norman, and to David Gee for yet another great cover. And to my son, Xander, for always being there and giving this book its first read on very short notice.